THE BABY-SITTERS CLUB
titles in Large-Print Editions:

Poor Mallory!
Ann M. Martin

Gareth Stevens Publishing
MILWAUKEE

For a free color catalog describing Gareth Stevens' list of high-quality books, call 1-800-542-2595 (USA) or 1-800-461-9120 (Canada). Gareth Stevens' Fax: (414) 225-0377.

Library of Congress Cataloging-in-Publication Data

Martin, Ann M., 1955-
    Poor Mallory!/by Ann M. Martin.
        p. cm. — (The Baby-sitters Club; #39)
        Summary: Mallory, whose family is suddenly short of money, takes a
    baby-sitting job and needs the help of the Baby-sitters Club in adjusting
    to her new employers' wealth.
        ISBN 0-8368-1419-3
        [1. Money—Fiction. 2. Wealth—Fiction. 3. Babysitters—Fiction.
    4. Clubs—Fiction.] I. Title. II. Series: Martin, Ann M., 1955-
    Baby-sitters Club; #39.
    PZ7.M3567585Po   1995
    [Fic]—dc20   95-21016

Published by Gareth Stevens, Inc., 1555 North RiverCenter Drive, Suite 201, Milwaukee, Wisconsin 53212 in large print by arrangement with Scholastic Inc., 555 Broadway, New York, New York 10012.

Cover art by Hodges Soileau.

Printed in the United States of America

1 2 3 4 5 6 7 8 9 99 98 97 96 95

*This book is for
Bonnie Black,
who keeps things running smoothly.
Thank you.*

CHAPTER 1

"*Underwear! Underwear!*" I sang. "*How I itch in my woolly underwear. Oh, how I wish I'd gottennnn*" (I held the note for as long as I could) "*a pair of cotton, so I wouldn't itch everywhere.*" I turned to Jessi Ramsey, my best friend. "Hit it, Jessi!" I cried.

Jessi picked up the song. "*BVDs make me sneeze, when the breeze from the trees hits my knees.*" (We were beginning to giggle.) "*Oh, I'm itching!*" Jessi managed to continue. "*Oh, how I'm itching, in my gosh-darn, bing-bang woolly underwear — hey!*"

"That's it! You got it!" I said. "That's the whole song."

"Your brothers know the weirdest songs," commented Jessi as we walked along. School was over. We had survived another day of sixth grade at Stoneybrook Middle School (or SMS).

I am Mallory Pike, better known as Mal. And Jessi is really Jessica, except she's *only* known as Jessi. Most days, when school is over, we walk home together, but just partway. After a couple of blocks we branch off, Jessi going in one direction and I in another.

"Want to come over this afternoon?" I asked Jessi. "The triplets" (they are three of my four brothers) "will teach you the song about Johnny Rebeck and his sausage-making machine."

"I'd *like* to come over," replied Jessi, "but I'm baby-sitting for Charlotte Johanssen. I'll see you at the Baby-sitters Club meeting at five-thirty, though, okay?"

"Okay," I replied.

We had reached our parting place. Jessi pretended, as she always does, that we were parting forever. She put the back of one hand to her forehead and began to moan. "Parting is such sweet sorrow," she said in this wispy voice.

"Will we ever pass this way again?" I asked her.

"Yeah, tomorrow," Jessi answered, and we laughed. "See you later," she said.

"Later!" I called to her.

I walked the rest of the way home by myself. Under my breath I sang, *"Oh, Mr. Johnny Re-*

beck, how could you be so mean? I told you you'd be sorry for inventing that machine. Now all the neighbors' cats and dogs will never more be seen — for they've all been ground to sausages in Johnny Rebeck's machine." Suddenly, I realized just what, exactly, I was singing about. "Ew, gross!" I said out loud. And then I wondered where my brothers had learned their weird songs. Probably at day camp when they were little.

When I reached my house, I shifted my book bag from one hand to the other and ran across our front lawn. We live in a medium-sized house in an average neighborhood in Stoneybrook, Connecticut, a small town. Sometimes I wish our house were just a little bigger. That's because I have seven brothers and sisters. We could really use the extra space. My brothers share one bedroom (two sets of bunk beds), my sister Vanessa and I share another room, and my two youngest sisters, Claire and Margo, share a third room. (My parents have the fourth bedroom. It isn't very big.)

"Hi, Mom!" I called as I opened the front door of our house. I took off my jacket and hung it in the coat closet. "Mom?" I called again. "Mom?"

"She's upstairs," said Claire, emerging from the kitchen. Claire is only five and goes to

3

kindergarten in the mornings, so she comes home from school before the rest of us do. "She's lying down," Claire added.

"Is she sick?" I asked in alarm.

"Nooo, but . . ." Claire trailed off.

"But what?" I asked her.

"We came home from school and the phone was ringing and Mommy answered it and she kept saying, 'Oh, no,' and then she hung up and she said she had a headache and she went to her room." Claire said this in a small explosion of words.

"Hmm," I replied. "Well, I'll go upstairs and see what's wrong." I wasn't too worried. If something really awful had happened, like if one of my grandparents had died or if Dad had been in an accident, Mom would be racing around *doing* things, not lying on her bed.

"Mom?" I called. I was standing in the upstairs hallway and the door to her room was ajar.

"Mallory?" Mom replied. "You can come in, honey."

I pushed open the door. Mom was sitting on the edge of her bed.

"I was just getting ready to come downstairs," she said.

"Oh. . . . Mom, what's wrong?"

4

Mom sighed. "I might as well tell you. And we should probably warn your brothers and sisters this afternoon, too."

Warn them? About what? This sounded dangerous. I replayed what Claire had told me. My mother had obviously gotten bad news over the phone. Had her *doctor* called? Was Mom sick? Maybe she'd heard those awful words: We have your test results, Mrs. Pike, and they don't look good.

"Are you *sick?*" I cried.

"Oh, no," said Mom. "It's nothing like that. Look, I'll tell you first, and then you can help me tell the others as they come home from school."

"Okay," I said.

"Well . . . well, it's the company your father works for," Mom began. (Dad is a corporate lawyer for a big firm in Stamford, Connecticut, which is not far from Stoneybrook.) "You know that it hasn't been doing well."

I nodded. Dad had been talking about that lately.

"Apparently this morning the president announced that half of the employees will be asked to leave."

"You mean fired?" I exclaimed. "That won't happen to Dad."

"Your father thinks it might," said Mom.

"Pink slips have been appearing on desks ever since the announcement was made."

"Pink slips?" I repeated.

"A pink slip is notification that you're being asked to leave your job," Mom explained.

"Oh. . . . but Dad hasn't gotten one yet."

"No. He thinks he will, though. He hasn't been at the company as long as most of the top executives have."

"And I know what that means," I said. "It means he doesn't have seniority."

"Right, smarty-pants," said Mom, smiling finally. Then she sighed. "We better go downstairs. I hear voices and footsteps."

"And thuds," I added. "The triplets must be home."

I was right. The triplets were home. So was everyone else. And they were all in the kitchen fixing sloppy, disgusting after-school snacks. There were Byron, Adam, and Jordan, who are ten; Vanessa, who's nine; Nicky, who's eight; Margo, who's seven; and Claire, who's five. (I'm eleven.)

Mom waited until everyone had fixed a snack and was sitting at the table in the kitchen. I joined my brothers and sisters, but I didn't feel like eating.

"Kids?" said Mom.

"Yeah?" replied Byron, just as Adam flicked

a Cheerio at Nicky, which caused Nicky to laugh and snort milk up his nose.

"Kids, this is serious," said Mom.

The giggling stopped. The eating stopped. Everyone faced our mother. Then she repeated what she had told me upstairs. I tried to help the little kids understand what she was saying.

"That's silly," scoffed Vanessa. "Dad's job is important."

"Yeah, he won't get fired," said Jordan.

"What's a pink slip?" asked Claire. "I don't get it."

Mom explained again, patiently.

"I *want* Daddy to get a pink slip!" exclaimed Claire. "If he didn't have to go to work, then he could stay at home and play with me."

"Jerk," said Adam. "If he doesn't work, how are we going to get money?"

"Yeah, we need money to buy food and clothes and stuff," said Nicky.

Claire finally began to look worried, so I said, "But we have a savings account, don't we, Mom? We could use the money that's in the bank."

"We do have a savings account," Mom answered, "but there's not a whole lot in it. We'll run through it pretty quickly trying to pay the mortgage and other bills every month, and putting food on this table for ten people. Besides, the money is supposed to be a college fund for you kids.''

My brothers and sisters and I looked at each other.

Finally Jordan said again, "Dad's not going to get fired."

"Yeah, we don't know that, Mom," I added. I looked at my watch. "It's after three-thirty. In fact, it's almost four. Don't you think Dad would know by now?"

Mom shrugged. "Not necessarily."

"But his job is im*por*tant," said Vanessa again.

"The company has other lawyers," Mom countered, "and they're all a lot older than your father. Look, I don't want Dad to get fired any more than you do. I'm just preparing you for what might happen, for what we might hear when Dad comes home tonight."

"If Daddy got fired," Claire began thoughtfully, "what would — what would change? I'm not sure . . . "

"We would have to be very careful with our money," said Mom. "We couldn't buy extras or go on trips. And your dad would stay at home and look for a new job. He wouldn't be happy about that," she added.

"Why not?" asked Margo.

"Because looking for a new job, especially

when you've been fired, is not easy. Dad will have to hear people say no to him a lot. He might start applying for jobs that are below the level of the one he's got now, and people still might say no. He'll call companies and hear other people say that there aren't any jobs at all. It would be like going over to your friends' houses and hearing each one of them say they don't want to play with you."

"Ooh," said Claire softly. That had hit home.

Margo looked as stricken as Claire.

"Anyway," said Mom, getting to her feet, "this might not happen. Your father may walk through the door tonight as happy as a clam. But I want you to be prepared if he doesn't."

"Okay," said my brothers and sisters and I.

I retreated to my room. I needed to think. In terms of "extras," what would those things be that we couldn't buy anymore? New clothes? What would happen if we outgrew our old clothes? Hand-me-downs only last so long. And I'm the oldest. There's no one in our family to hand clothes down to me. When we went to the grocery, what could we buy? We probably wouldn't be able to buy ice cream or cookies or any fun stuff. Would we have to get food stamps? I had always heard about food stamps but I wasn't sure what they were or how they worked — just that they were supposed to help people "stretch their food dollars."

I wanted desperately to talk to Jessi. I always call my best friend when a crisis arises — or when something good happens. But Jessi had said she was sitting for Charlotte that afternoon. The members of the Baby-sitters Club (I'll explain about the BSC later) try not to call each other when we're working. We take our sitting jobs seriously.

But I decided that this was an emergency.

CHAPTER 2

I went into Mom and Dad's bedroom, sat in the flowered armchair, and dialed the Johanssens' number.

Jessi answered the phone professionally. "Hello, Johanssens' residence."

"Hi, Jessi. It's me," I said.

"Mal, what's wrong?" (My voice must have given away my feelings.)

"Mom's really worried," I told Jessi. "She and Dad are pretty sure that Dad's going to get fired today."

"*Fired?* Lose his *job? Your* father?" (I guess I don't need to point out that Jessi was shocked.)

"Yeah," I said. I explained to Jessi what was happening at Dad's company. Then I added, "I'm really sorry to interrupt you while you're baby-sitting."

"Oh, that's okay," Jessi answered. "Charlotte's doing her homework. She doesn't even need help." (Charlotte is very bright. She skipped a grade in school and is still at the top of her class.)

"I'm just so worried," I told Jessi. "It's bad enough to lose your job. But it's especially bad when you have eight kids, a wife — and a hamster — to support."

"Listen, I know this is easy for me to say, but try not to worry. Maybe your dad *won't* lose his job."

"That's what I keep hoping," I answered. Then I sighed. "Oh, well. I'll let you go. I'll see you at the meeting."

We hung up and I went to my bedroom and flopped on my bed. I was hoping for privacy, which meant I was hoping Vanessa would stay out. Since we share a bedroom, I can't force her to stay out, but sometimes Vanessa can tell when I want to be alone, and then she stays away without being asked.

Anyway, I seemed to have the room to myself, so I closed my eyes and thought of Jessi and my other friends, all members of the Baby-sitters Club. If Dad really did lose his job, I had a feeling I would need my friends. I would need them to stick by me, and I was pretty sure they would. We've stuck together during other bad times, like when Claudia's grandmother died, and when Stacey's parents got divorced.

I guess I should tell you about my friends, so you'll know the kind of people I'm talking about. I'll start with Jessi, since she's my best friend. Jessi and I are alike in lots of ways. First of all, we're both eleven. We're the two youngest members of the BSC. Everyone else in the club is thirteen and in eighth grade at Stoneybrook Middle School. Jessi and I are also both the oldest in our families, although Jessi doesn't have nearly as many brothers and sisters as I do. She just has Becca (short for Rebecca), who is eight, and her baby brother, Squirt, whose real name is John Philip Ramsey, Jr. Jessi and I feel that, although we're the oldest in our families, our parents still treat us like babies sometimes. Our friend Claudia says eleven is a hard age because your parents can't decide whether you *are* a baby or not. For instance, our parents *did* let us get our ears pierced, but Mom and Dad won't let me get contacts yet, so I still have to wear my glasses, which I hate. Plus, I wear braces on my teeth. They're the plastic kind, which don't look too bad, but I don't think I'm particularly attractive these days. Hey — if Dad loses his job, maybe the dentist will have to remove my braces! (I knew that was a mean thought, but it just goes to show how badly I want to get rid of my metal mouth, which is what the kids at school call it, even though it's really a plastic mouth.)

Anyway, Jessi and I both like to read, especially horse stories, and especially the ones by Marguerite Henry. And I *love* to write and draw pictures. I keep a journal in which I write down my innermost thoughts and feelings. I write stories, too, and illustrate them. Someday I hope to become an author and illustrator of children's books. Jessi likes to write, too, and recently I convinced her to keep a journal like mine. But her passion is dancing. Jessi is a ballerina. She dances *en pointe* (that means *on toe*), and she takes lessons at this special school in Stamford that she had to audition just to get into. She has performed onstage lots of times and has even had leading roles, or whatever they're called in ballet.

One difference between Jessi and me is our skin color. She's black and I'm white. This doesn't matter to us or to our BSC friends, but it's been hard to ignore since, when the Ramseys first moved here, some people were not very nice to them. For reasons I haven't figured out entirely, they didn't want another black family in our community, which is almost all white. (Jessi is the only black kid in the entire sixth grade.)

Let's see. What else about Jessi? She's pretty (I think), she has long eyelashes, and long, *long* dancer's legs. She's a good student. And she lives with her parents, her brother and sister, and her Aunt Cecelia, who helps run the house since both Mr. and Mrs. Ramsey work.

Okay. On to the other BSC members. The president of the club is Kristy Thomas. (Jessi and I are junior officers, since we're still too young to baby-sit at night.) Kristy has the most incredible family. (Or as she would say, the most dibble family. *Dibble* is short for *incredible*. My friends love to make up words. Another word meaning *dibble* is *distant*. The opposite of *dibble* and *distant* is *stale*!) Kristy's family is as big as mine, but all mixed up. Kristy lives with her mom; her two older brothers, Charlie and Sam; her little brother, David Michael; her stepfather, Watson; her adopted Vietnamese sister, Emily Michelle; and her grandmother, Nannie. Every other week, Watson's children, who live with their mother here in Stoney-brook, come to stay for the weekend. They are Karen and Andrew (seven and almost five) and they're Kristy's stepsister and stepbrother.

The way Kristy acquired this family is that her father walked out right after David Michael was born, leaving Mrs. Thomas to raise four kids. In those days, the Thomases lived across the street from Claudia Kishi (BSC vice-president) and next door to Mary Anne Spier (BSC secretary and Kristy's best friend). Mrs. Thomas worked hard, finally began to date (to Kristy's dismay), and soon met Watson Brewer, whom she fell in love with — and married! Watson is a millionaire and has a huge house (okay, it's a mansion) on the other side of town, so he moved the Thomases from their cramped house into his gigantic house. Kristy adjusted pretty well, considering she didn't like Watson at first. But she's used to her new neighborhood and expanded family.

Kristy is a tomboy who loves sports. She even coaches a softball team called Kristy's Krushers. It's for kids who are too young or too scared to join Little League. Kristy dresses in a sort of tomboyish way, too. She usually wears jeans, sneakers, a turtleneck, and — in cool weather — a sweater. She likes this old baseball cap with a picture of a collie on it. I guess I have to say that, although Kristy's mother and stepfather would probably let her wear anything she wants, Kristy just doesn't care that much about clothes. She's a little less mature than her eighth-grade friends, although she does sort of have a boyfriend named Bart, who coaches a rival softball team — Bart's Bashers. (Bart lives in her neighborhood but goes to a private school.

Kristy and us BSC members go to public school.)

Kristy is the shortest kid in her class, has brown hair and brown eyes, and is the only older BSC member who doesn't wear a bra yet. She can be bossy and has a big mouth, but we all love Kristy. She's funny and creative and *great* with children.

As I mentioned before, Claudia Kishi is the club vice-president. She and Kristy are about as different as night and day. Claudia is also outgoing, but she doesn't have a big mouth, and she is *so dibbly* sophisticated and chic. She wears wild clothes like big hats; flowered vests over long shirts that belong to her father and which she leaves untucked; short black pants; and then, something just a little offbeat like penny loafers from the 1950s with white bobby socks. And her jewelry. It's the height of dibble-dom. She makes most of it herself — ceramic-bead necklaces and big dangly earrings, but in shapes you wouldn't expect. For example, in my ears I am allowed to wear studs or *very* tiny gold hoops. Period. Claudia might wear a monkey in one ear and a banana in the other. Also, one of her ears is doubly pierced, so she can wear a hoop and a stud or something in that ear, too. (By the way, Kristy does *not* have pierced ears and neither does Mary Anne.)

How does Claud make her jewelry? She's a fantastic artist, that's how. She is *really* talented. She can paint, draw, sculpt, make collages, you name it. And she takes pottery classes sometimes. Claud's other passions are eating junk food and reading Nancy Drew mysteries, neither of which her parents approve of, so Claud hides the books as well as Mallomars, potato chips, red hots, etc., all over her room.

Claud lives with her parents and her older sister, Janine. Janine is a certified genius. This is too bad for Claudia, since, although she's smart, she's a terrible student — and a worse speller. Her teachers say she could make better grades if she just applied herself, but Claud says she isn't interested. (Personally, I think that Claud is afraid to try harder because she'd find out that even if she did she still couldn't live up to Janine.)

Claudia is Japanese-American, and she is drop-dead gorgeous. She has this *long*, silky black hair, which she likes to fix in different ways. (And of course she has millions of bows and funky barrettes and stuff for it.) Her eyes are dark and almond-shaped, and her skin, despite her junk-food addiction, is perfectly clear.

Claud's best friend is Stacey McGill, who's the treasurer of the BSC. Stacey is just as sophisticated and chic as Claudia, if not more so. In fact, the other day, Claudia referred to Stacey as the Queen of Dibbleness. Stacey's family story is about as interesting as Kristy's. She grew up in big, glamorous New York City. Then, just before she was supposed to enter seventh grade there, her father's company transferred him to Connecticut, so Stacey and her parents moved to Stoneybrook. (Stacey's an only child.) The McGills had been here for less than a year when the company moved them *back* to New York. That was hard on everyone, but especially on Claudia and Stacey. In New York, the McGills' marriage began to fail, and before Stacey knew what had hit her, her parents announced that they were getting a divorce. Not only that, Mr. McGill wanted to stay in the city with his job, while Mrs. McGill wanted to move back to Stoneybrook. After a lot of thought, Stacey decided to live with her mother (were we ever glad!) but she visits her father in New York pretty often. Guess what. When Stacey and her mom returned to Stoneybrook, they had to find a new house to live in. That was because Jessi and her family had moved into the McGills' old house!

As I mentioned before, Stacey is as cool as Claud. She dresses in outfits that are just as wild, *and* she gets to perm her blonde hair sometimes. Plus, she likes to wear sparkly nail polish. And in her pierced ears, she often wears earrings that Claud has made for her.

Stacey is pretty, but as far as I'm concerned, too thin. This is probably because on top of her family problems, Stacey has a severe form of diabetes. That's a disease in which her pancreas doesn't make the right amount of something called insulin, which controls her blood sugar. Stacey can't eat sweets, except for controlled amounts of fruit, and she has to give herself injections (ew, ew, EW) of insulin every day. She also has to monitor her blood and eat only a certain number of calories each day. Poor Stace. Some people can control their diabetes with diet alone. They don't have to bother with injections (*EW*), or blood tests, or calorie-counting. But not Stacey. She has to be *very* careful or she could go into a diabetic coma. My friends and I are a little worried because Stacey hasn't been feeling too great lately. But she seems to be coping.

Two more members of the BSC are Mary Anne Spier and Dawn Schafer. Mary Anne, as I said, is the club secretary and Kristy's best friend. Mary Anne has another best friend, though, and that's Dawn. Like Stacey and Jessi, Dawn is a newcomer to Stoneybrook. (The rest of us were born here and grew up here.) Dawn moved to Connecticut from California in the middle of seventh grade. This was because her parents were getting a divorce, and Mrs. Schafer wanted to move back to the town in which she'd been raised — Stoneybrook. She brought Dawn and Dawn's younger brother, Jeff, with her, and they settled into a colonial farmhouse that has an actual secret passage in it! Soon, Dawn and Mary Anne became friends, and then, guess what they discovered. They found out that Dawn's mom and Mary Anne's dad had been high-school sweethearts. Since Mary Anne's mother had died when Mary Anne was just a baby, the girls decided to reintroduce their parents. And after dating practically forever, Mr. Spier and Mrs. Schafer got married — so Dawn and Mary Anne became stepsisters. And now Mary Anne, her father, and her kitten, Tigger, live in the Schafers' farmhouse. One sad thing is that Jeff moved back to California to live with his dad. He never adjusted to life in Connecticut. He's much happier in California.

Although Mary Anne and Dawn are best friends, they're pretty different people. Mary Anne is shy and has trouble showing her feelings, except when she cries, which is often. She is also very romantic and is the first BSC member to have a steady boyfriend. (Her boyfriend is Logan Bruno. He comes from Louisville, Kentucky, is nice and funny and understanding, and speaks with this great drawl.) Mary Anne's father used to be dibbly strict with her. He even picked out her clothes, so she dressed like a first-grader. Now he's loosened up, and so has Mary Anne. She dresses pretty well, especially since she and Dawn can trade clothes. Mary Anne is short, has brown eyes and brown hair, and looks like Kristy!

Dawn, on the other hand, is about as gorgeous as Claudia. Our California girl has LONG blonde hair and sparkly blue eyes. She's not shy like Mary Anne or a loudmouth like Kristy. She's just herself. She's very independent and dresses however she wants, which is usually casual but cool. Dawn is totally into health food, wouldn't touch meat with a ten-foot pole, and always refuses Claudia's candy. (This is nice for Stacey.) Dawn likes mysteries and ghost stories (so of course she *loves* the secret passage in her house, which may, by the way, be haunted). And she misses Jeff, her dad, and California. Luckily, though, she likes Stoneybrook and her new family.

So — those are my friends. The ones I would turn to in a crisis. For instance, if Dad lost his job. But that, I had decided, was not going to happen.

22

Apparently, my brothers and sisters had decided the same thing.

"See you at dinner," I said as I left for the BSC meeting. "We're going to hear good news then, aren't we, you guys?"

"Sure," replied Jordan.

"Of course," said Vanessa. "Dad would never get fired."

CHAPTER 3

I rode my bike to Claudia Kishi's house and arrived there at 5:20. BSC meetings start at five-thirty on the dot.

"Hi, Claud!" I said as I entered her room. I sounded pretty cheerful since I had convinced myself that my family had nothing to worry about.

"Hi," replied Claud. "What kind of snack do you want today?"

I went for the junkiest. "Mallomars," I said immediately.

"Good choice!" Claud must have been in a junky mood, too. "Now if I can just remember where I hid them . . ."

"In your hollow book?" I suggested.

"Nope. They don't fit in there. I've tried. Let me see. . . . Oh, yeah." Claud opened a drawer in her desk, found a key, used the key to open her jewelry box, and produced the promised Mallomars.

"How did you fit the Mallomars in there with all your jewelry?" I asked.

"I didn't. I had to take the jewelry out to make room. And I put it . . . Hmm. Oh, yeah. In my pencil case."

I was going to ask Claud where she had put the stuff that was in her pencil case, but I decided not to. Sometimes talking to Claud makes my head spin.

Anyway, the other club members were arriving. By 5:29, Stacey was in Claud's desk chair — backward, facing into the room, her arms draped over the rungs. Mary Anne, Dawn, and Claudia were sitting in a row on Claud's bed, leaning against the wall. Jessi and I were seated cross-legged on the floor, working on a paper-clip chain. And Kristy, ready to start the meeting, was sitting in Claud's director's chair, wearing a visor, a pencil stuck over one ear, with the club notebook open in her lap.

As the numbers on Claudia's digital alarm clock changed from 5:29 to 5:30, Kristy cleared her throat. Then she said, "Attention! This meeting of the Baby-sitters Club will now come to order."

As you might have guessed, Claud's bedroom is the official headquarters of the BSC. We meet there three times a week, on Mondays, Wednesdays, and Fridays from five-thirty until six, and we take job calls from people who need to line up baby-sitters. How do people know about our meetings and that they should call us at those times? Because we advertise. Maybe I better explain things a little.

The original idea for the Baby-sitters Club was Kristy's. She got the idea back at the beginning of seventh grade, just after Stacey had moved to Stoneybrook. In those days, Kristy's mom had not yet married Watson Brewer, the Thomases still lived on Bradford Court across the street from Claudia and next door to Mary Anne and her dad, and Kristy and her older brothers were responsible for baby-sitting for David Michael after school. But of course an afternoon came when Kristy, Sam, and Charlie were all busy, so Mrs. Thomas had to phone for a baby-sitter and she had to make a lot of calls because no one seemed to be available.

Mom is wasting her time, thought Kristy. And that's when she got her great idea. Wouldn't it be wonderful if her mother could make just one call and reach a lot of sitters at once? So Kristy invited Mary Anne and Claudia to form the Baby-sitters Club with her. The first thing the girls decided, though, was that they really needed at least four members, so they asked Stacey to join the club, too. Stacey and Claudia had met in school and were already becoming friends.

26

After the girls decided when they were going to meet, they had to decide where to meet. The answer was obvious: in Claudia's room, because she has not only her own phone, but her own phone number. And then the club members began advertising. They even placed an ad in the *Stoneybrook News*. And during their very first meeting people called them needing baby-sitters. (Well, actually one person needed a dog-sitter, but that's a long story.) Anyway, by January of that school year, the BSC was getting so much business that when Dawn moved to town, the girls invited her to join the club. Then, at the beginning of eighth grade (sixth grade for Jessi and me), Stacey moved back to New York. So Kristy, Claudia, Mary Anne, and Dawn asked Jessi and me to join the BSC. Of course, when Stacey returned to Stoneybrook after her parents split up, we let her right back in the club. Now the BSC has seven members and that's plenty. Claud's room is getting crowded!

As president of the club, Kristy runs our meetings (quite officially). She also thinks up ways to keep the club efficient — and creative. For instance, the club record book, the club notebook, and Kid-Kits were all Kristy's ideas. (The record book is Mary Anne's department, so I'll describe that later.) The notebook is like a diary. It's where we write up each and every job we go on. This is something of a pain, but we all agree that it's necessary and helpful. See, each of us is responsible for reading the notebook once a week. That way we find out what happened on our friends' sitting jobs. We learn how they solved baby-sitting problems, and we keep up with the children our club sits for regularly. It's always useful to know if a kid has developed a fear, is having trouble at school, or anything else that's new or unusual. Then there are Kid-Kits. I just love mine. When Kristy got the idea for Kid-Kits, each of us made one. We found cardboard cartons, decorated them with paint, fabric, and other art supplies belonging to Claudia, then filled the boxes with our old books, toys, and games from home, as well as some new, store-bought things, such as coloring books, Magic Markers, construction paper, and stickers. When we go on sitting jobs, we sometimes take the Kid-Kits along. Children love them! They don't even care that half the toys are old. There's just something appealing about playing with toys that are new *to them*. I have to brag a little here and say that the Kid-Kits have helped make us pretty popular baby-sitters! Anyway, you can see why Kristy, with her big ideas, is such a good president for our club.

Claudia is the vice-president mostly because three times a week her room is invaded for club meetings, and her junk food is eaten. But she also gets stuck taking calls that, for one reason or another, come in while we're not holding a meeting. Then she has to schedule those jobs herself.

The person who's *really* in charge of scheduling, though, is Mary Anne. As secretary, that's one of her main jobs. Also, she's in charge of the record book. The record book is where we keep track of our clients, their addresses and phone numbers, the rates they pay, how much money we earn (that's actually Stacey's department), and — most important — our schedules. Every time one of our clients calls, Mary Anne opens the record book to the appointment pages and checks to see who's free to take the job. Poor Mary Anne has to remember an awful lot of things, such as when Jessi has ballet classes, I have orthodontist appointments, or Kristy has a Krushers practice. But Mary Anne is organized and precise (she has neat handwriting, too), and she's great at the job. No one could do it better than she does.

As club treasurer, Stacey records the money each of us earns. (This is just for our own information. We don't divide up our earnings or anything.) She also collects dues from us each Monday. The dues go into the club treasury (a manila envelope), and Stacey doles it out as needed: to pay Charlie Thomas to drive Kristy to and from club meetings now that she lives on the other side of town, to help Claudia pay her phone bill, to buy supplies for the Kid-Kits when things run out or get used up, and for fun things such as club parties or sleepovers! Stacey is a very good treasurer. She's a whiz at math, and she loves money, even if it's really club money. Sometimes we even have a little trouble getting her to part with it. But in the end, she always does.

Dawn is our alternate officer. Her job is to be able to fill in for anybody who might miss a meeting. In other words, she has know how to schedule jobs, keep track of money, etc. She's like an understudy in a play. Since most of us don't miss meetings very often, though, she doesn't usually have anything special to do, so we let her answer the phone a lot.

Jessi and I are junior officers, which simply means that we're too young to take nighttime jobs, unless we're sitting for our own families. But we're still a big help to the club. Taking on a lot of afternoon and weekend jobs frees the older members for the nighttime ones.

Guess what. Technically, there are two other club members. I haven't mentioned them yet because they don't come to meetings. They're our associate members, and they're people we can call on to take a job if none of the rest of us can take it. Believe it or not, that does happen sometimes. Our associate members are Shannon Kilbourne, a friend of Kristy's (she lives across the street from Kristy), and . . . Logan Bruno, Mary Anne's boyfriend! He's a terrific baby-sitter.

Our Wednesday meeting was underway. I found that, for short periods of time, I was able to forget that bad news might be waiting for me at home. I tried to concentrate on the meeting.

"Any club business?" asked Kristy.

"Jenny Prezzioso's going to be a big sister!" announced Dawn. I could tell she'd been holding that secret in for a long time, probably since Monday night when she had sat at the Prezziosos'.

"Mrs. Prezzioso is going to have a baby and you didn't even tell *me?*" exclaimed Mary Anne. (Mary Anne is the only one of us who tolerates Jenny very well. Jenny is a four-year-old spoiled brat. I wondered how she would react to being a sister and having to share everything — including her parents.)

"It was worth keeping the secret to see the expressions on your faces," Dawn said. "And guess what. The Prezziosos already know what the baby will be. Mrs. P. had a test done. The baby's going to be a — "

"Wait! Don't tell!" I cried. "I don't know

about the rest of you, but I want to be surprised."

"Me, too," said everyone except Mary Anne.

"I'll tell you at home tonight," Dawn said to her stepsister.

"Okay," agreed Mary Anne.

The phone rang then and Dawn answered it. "Hello, Baby-sitters Club. . . . Oh, hi! . . . For a whole month? . . . Oh, okay. I'll check with Mary Anne and call you right back." Dawn hung up the phone. "That was Mrs. Delaney," she said. (The Delaneys live in Kristy's ritzy new neighborhood, right next door to Shannon Kilbourne. There are two Delaney kids — Amanda, who's eight, and Max, who's six. Kristy used to call them the snobs, since they were so bossy and mean when the club first began sitting for them, but now she's changed her mind. She can handle the Delaneys.) "Mrs. Delaney wants to go back to work," Dawn told us, "so she's taking a refresher course in real estate. She needs a sitter on Mondays, Wednesdays, and Fridays from three-thirty till five for the next *month*."

"Boy, that might be hard to schedule," said Mary Anne, looking at the appointment pages in the record book. "No, wait. You could do it, Mal, and so could you, Kristy."

"You take it, Kristy," I said immediately. "It makes much more sense since you live in the Delaneys' neighborhood."

So Kristy took the job. I knew she considered that particular meeting a huge success.

CHAPTER
4

When the meeting was over, the BSC members trickled out of Claud's house.

"Any word?" Jessi whispered to me as we unchained our bicycles from the Kishis' lamppost.

I shook my head, glad that Jessi hadn't said anything about my dad's job at the meeting. She's a good enough friend to know when to keep quiet. "Dad should be home by the time I get home, though," I said. "I'll call you tonight to tell you whether the news is good or bad."

"Okay," replied Jessi. "I'll keep my fingers crossed. I'm *sure* the news will be good. Talk to you later."

"Later!" I called as we both rode off.

I pedaled along in the semidark. Good news, good news, good news, I said to myself in time to the pedaling.

When I reached my street, I picked up

speed. (Good-news-good-news-good-news.) And when I reached my driveway, I picked up even more speed. (Goodnewsgoodnewsgoodnews.) I was riding so fast that I nearly crashed into Dad's car as I sped into the garage.

Calm down, just calm down, I told myself.

I entered our house through the garage door. The rec room was silent and empty. So I ran upstairs to the living room. Everyone was sitting there, either on the couch or chairs, or on the floor.

No one had to tell me what the news was. I could see for myself.

"Oh, Dad," I said, letting out a breath.

"I'm sorry," said Dad simply.

"Hey, you don't have to apologize," I told him quickly. "It wasn't your fault."

"He got a pink slip," Claire spoke up. She was sitting on the floor, playing with Vanessa's hair. "He got it at five o'clock."

"Those stinkers!" I exploded. "Why did they wait so long to tell you? Why didn't they give out all the slips in the morning, instead of driving people crazy making them wait all day?"

"I don't know." Dad sighed. "Maybe they were still making decisions about who should go and who should stay. Those aren't easy decisions."

"Well, I still think the people who run your company are really stale."

"Look," said Dad, sounding cross, "I got fired and that's that. I don't want to spend all night discussing it."

"*Okay. Sorry,*" I replied. I was taken aback. Mom and Dad usually don't talk that way. My brothers and sisters and I do sometimes, but not our parents. And especially not Dad. He's a sensitive, gentle person.

"Come on," said Mom. "Let's have dinner."

"Is it okay to eat? Shouldn't we be saving our food for when we really need it?" asked Nicky. He wasn't being sassy. He *meant* it.

"For pity's sake, we aren't destitute," answered Dad.

"What's 'dessatoot'?" Claire whispered to me as we followed Mom and Dad into the kitchen. I felt bad for her. I knew she was whispering because she didn't want Dad to hear her and get mad at *her*.

"Destitute," I corrected her, "and it means as poor as you can get."

"Very, *very* poor?" whispered Claire.

"Right. Very, very poor. And we aren't very, very poor," (yet, I thought) "so don't worry, okay?"

"Okay."

Dinner that night was gloomy, as you might imagine. At first, no one knew what to say.

So we didn't say anything. Then finally Mom spoke up. (Sometimes it's nice to have a mother who speaks her mind. Other times it is dibbly horrible.)

"Okay, everybody," said Mom. "Heads up, eyes on me." She sounded like a teacher, but I think she just didn't want us looking ashamed and embarrassed. We looked at her. Even Dad looked at her. "We've got a problem here," said Mom.

"Duh," muttered Jordan.

"I heard that," Mom said, then continued by saying, "We are a family."

"We are the world, we are the people," sang Jordan.

"Jordan!" bellowed Dad. (He didn't need to say another word.)

"We are a family," Mom repeated, "and we will stick together and work together and everything will be fine. I want you to under-stand what I mean by work together," she went on.

"You mean like in the garden?" interrupted Margo.

"Not exactly," said Mom. "I mean, doing what is asked of you, since we're going to have to make some changes. First of all, no extras. That means new clothes only if it's a *necessity*. If it's not a necessity, you wait, or you ask a brother or sister — nicely — if you can borrow something. It means no new toys, because we've got plenty already. It means no trips, and it means that your father or I will do the grocery shopping and we won't hear complaints about what we buy." (I knew it, I thought. This was the end of the junk food.) "Furthermore," continued Mom, "I will be going to work."

"*You* will?" cried Adam. The idea was foreign to him.

"Yup," Mom answered. "I can type and use word processors, so I'm going to register with an agency to do temporary work. That means," she said, "that I won't have a steady job, I'll just be working at companies whenever and wherever I'm needed, and that means that some days I'll be working and some days I won't, and *that* means, Mallory, that if I'm at work and your father needs to go on a job interview, I'll ask you to baby-sit — for free. Do you understand?"

"Sure," I replied. I was glad I could help out.

"Oh, another thing," said Mom. "I hate to tell you this, but no allowances until we're back on our feet. We need every penny."

"No allowances?" repeated Byron. "Aw, *man.*"

"Sorry, kiddo," said Mom.

"That's okay," Byron replied, glancing at Dad.

During this entire discussion, Dad hadn't said a word (except to chew out Jordan). Now I studied him and decided he looked almost angry. Why? I wondered. I thought we were all being pretty cooperative and accepting. Mom was going to get work, I had said I'd baby-sit for free (and without any help — Mom usually insists on *two* sitters at our house), and my brothers and sisters and I had barely griped about cutting back or losing our allowances. I would have thought Dad would be proud, or at least pleased, but he certainly didn't look as if he *felt* proud or pleased. Which made *me* feel confused.

I was so deep in thought that when Dad said, "Kids?" I jumped a mile.

"Yeah?" we replied.

"I'll be in charge when your mother's at . . . at work," he said gruffly. "I'll expect you to listen to me and behave."

Why wouldn't we? I wondered.

"I'll probably only work a couple of days a week," said Mom apologetically.

"Right," said Dad shortly.

Next to me, Claire became wiggly. I nudged her with my elbow. For some reason it seemed important for us to be model kids, and I realized why. I didn't want to upset Dad any further.

I felt afraid.

When our torturous dinner was finally over, nobody scattered, as we usually do. Instead, we helped clear the table and clean up the kitchen. Then my brothers and sisters and I crept to our rooms, leaving Mom and Dad downstairs.

"You guys?" I said softly, standing in the hallway, where I knew everyone could hear me. "Come into my room for a sec."

In a minute, the eight of us were jammed into Vanessa's and my bedroom, somber-faced.

"Okay," I began. "I call to order a meeting of the Pike Club."

Claire brightened. She likes the idea of clubs and wishes she could belong to the BSC. "What's the Pike Club?" she asked.

"It's us," I replied. "The eight of us. And we're going to meet sometimes while Dad is out of work to talk about things."

"What kind of things?" Nicky wanted to know.

"Well, ways we can help save money. . . . And things we're afraid of," I tossed in, off-handedly. I knew we were all afraid of things we hadn't mentioned yet.

"I'm scared of Daddy," said Margo in a small voice. "He yelled tonight. And I think he's mad at Mommy."

"He *sounded* like he was mad at Mommy," I said slowly, "but I think maybe he's mad at himself. Or ashamed. Even though he shouldn't be."

"Well," said Byron, "let's think of some other ways to save money."

"Yeah!" cried Nicky. "Like not leave on lights when we don't need them."

"Good idea," I agreed. "We could probably cut our electricity bill way back just by being careful. Don't leave *any*thing on unless you really need it. We're always forgetting and leaving the power to the stereo on. And we can watch less TV and not use the stereo or our radios too often."

"We should use dish towels instead of paper towels," added Vanessa. "Then we wouldn't have to buy paper towels."

"And only one Kleenex instead of two when we blow our noses," said Claire.

I smiled. "These are all terrific ideas. See what happens when the Pike Club meets? We can think of plenty of ways to cut back." I looked at my brothers and sisters, who seemed relaxed. That was nice.

The first meeting of the Pike Club broke up

about ten minutes later. Most of us had homework to do, including me. But instead of starting it, I called Jessi.

"My dad lost his job," I whispered to her. (I didn't want my family to know that I was already spreading our bad news.)

"He *did?!*" Jessi squeaked. "I don't believe it. How stale." She paused. "Mal? Is there anything I can do?"

I thought for a moment. "Not really, I guess. Just . . . just let me lean on you when I need to. My brothers and sisters are all leaning on *me.*"

"Boy," and Jessi. "If they lean on you and you lean on me, I might fall over."

"Please don't," I said, giggling.

"I won't. You know I'm here," Jessi told me seriously.

"I know. Thanks, Jessi. I'll see you tomorrow. Good night."

" 'Night, Mal."

CHAPTER 5

Friday afternoon arrived. It was time for the next meeting of the Baby-sitters Club. Two days had passed since the last meeting and since my dad lost his job, but the days felt more like years. Mom had registered with the temping agency, but they hadn't called her with a job yet. And my dad had launched right into his search for a new job. He worked so hard at it that he was making a job out of looking for a job.

However, my parents didn't seem much happier than they had on Wednesday night. Breakfast and dinner were agonizing times. Dad was gruff and cross, Mom was constantly apologizing for him, and the rest of us didn't know what to do or say, so mostly we were silent. Neither Mom nor Dad seemed to notice the money-saving campaign that my brothers and sisters and I had started, though the house was noticeably quiet with the TV, stereo, and radios off most of the time. Mom and Dad didn't even say anything when we washed the supper dishes by hand on Thursday night, so as not to use up electricity by running the dishwasher. I think Mom and Dad were dazed.

I called Jessi with great regularity to report on things.

By Friday, my friends knew what happened. Mom and Dad had not said to keep Dad's job loss a secret, and anyway, secrets don't last long in the BSC. So when I reached Claud's room that afternoon I was greeted by a chorus of, "How were things this afternoon?" and, "How's your dad doing?"

"Okay," I had time to answer before Claud's clock turned to 5:30 and Kristy called our meeting to order.

"Any club business?" Kristy asked, then immediately answered her own question. "I move that we let Mal have the job at the Delaneys', that is, if Mrs. Delaney approves. You haven't sat for the Delaneys, have you, Mal?"

I shook my head. Why was Kristy giving me the job?

"I second the motion," said Claudia.

"I third it," said Dawn, and we laughed.

"Just a minute, you guys. What's going on?"

I asked. "Kristy, how come you can't take the job with Amanda and Max?"

"Oh, I can take it. But I think you need it more than I do." Kristy stopped abruptly, probably wondering if she'd just blurted out something she shouldn't have said. "You're not offended, are you?" she asked.

"No," I replied. "Just, um, surprised. And — And — " I didn't know what else to say except, "Thank you, Kristy." Then I thought of something. "Wait a sec! Don't call Mrs. Delaney yet. How am I going to get to your neighborhood every day, Kristy? I can't ride my bike that far, and I can't ask my parents for a ride, either." (It had been Jordan's idea to save on gas.)

"No problem. I've got it all worked out," Kristy answered. She grinned at me from under her visor. "Mrs. Delaney needs a sitter on Mondays, Wednesdays, and Fridays, right?"

"Right," I said.

"And those are club meeting days, right?"

"Right."

"Okay, so three times a week you'll take the bus home with me, go over to the Delaneys', and then ride with Charlie and me to Claudia's. Charlie can even drop you off at your house after the meetings, since you won't have your bike."

"I think we should let Mal have as many sitting jobs as she can handle," added Claudia. "Tuesdays, Thursdays, weekends. Whatever jobs come in."

"Yeah, Mal has first dibs on daytime jobs," said Stacey. "That's fair."

"Mal?" asked Jessi. "Mal?"

I hadn't said anything because I was desperately trying not to cry. I swallowed hard and finally found my voice. "Thanks," I managed to say. "This is — I mean, you guys are — "

"Don't! Stop!" exclaimed Mary Anne. "In a few seconds, *I'm* going to cry!"

"Oh, lord," said Claud.

"I'll call Mrs. Delaney," Kristy spoke up in her most businesslike voice.

There. That was good. The meeting began to feel more normal.

Mrs. Delaney agreed to the change in sitters without even asking questions. She trusts the BSC.

So the job became mine. By that time, I was more in control. (So was Mary Anne.) "This is dibbly great," I said. "I've decided I'm going to give all of my baby-sitting money to Mom and Dad to help with the groceries and stuff. Well, I'll give them most of it, anyway. I might save a little for myself in case I need something. Then I won't have to ask them to buy it for me."

The phone rang then. It was Mrs. Prezzioso needing a sitter for the following Thursday afternoon. Mary Anne gave me the job after saying, "Only if you really want it, Mal. I know how you feel about Jenny. I'll take the job if you don't want to go to the Prezziosos'."

"No, I'll go. I can't afford to be a baby now. I'll put up with Jenny." I felt like a soldier volunteering to cross enemy lines or do something else equally dangerous.

So I got the job with Jenny. Wow! I thought. I'll be rich! Then I paused. No, I wouldn't. And neither would my parents when I turned my pay over to them. Baby-sitting money was not going to feed ten people.

The phone rang several more times, and several more jobs were scheduled.

After the last call, Claud waited a moment to see if the phone would ring again. When it didn't, she reached behind her pillow and pulled out a bag of Fritos, which she passed around.

"Hey, Jessi, Mal," she said. "You know what happened at lunch today?"

"What?" we asked. (Jessi and I eat lunch with the sixth-graders. The other club members eat with the eighth-graders during a later period. They all sit together. Sometimes Logan joins them.)

"Dori Wallingford fainted."

"You're kidding!" exclaimed Jessi. But I wasn't listening. I couldn't help thinking about what had happened during *my* lunch period.

"Mal? . . . Mal?" Claud was saying. "Earth to Mal."

"Oh, sorry." I must have really zoned out.

"Anything wrong?" asked Dawn.

I glanced at Jessi. *She* knew what was wrong.

"It's just that . . . well, at lunch today, um — " I began.

"Yeah?" said Mary Anne.

"Nan White — Do you know her?" I asked my friends.

"I do, sort of," said Kristy. "She isn't the nicest person in the world. She likes to put people down. Especially — don't take this the wrong way, Mal — but especially people who aren't good at fighting back."

"Well, she chose the right person," I said. "Jessi and I were eating lunch, minding our own business, when Nan came up to me and said, 'I heard your father got fired. What'd he do? Steal from his company?' "

"I hoped you denied that," said Stacey, looking astonished.

"I tried to. But Nan was with Janet O'Neal," I replied.

"A bad combination," added Jessi.

"Yeah," I agreed. "And the two of them stood there and laughed and said that *their* fathers had never been fired. And then they sat down with Valerie and Rachel, and all *four* of them began talking about me. I know they were talking about me because they kept looking over at our table. They weren't very subtle. And they laughed a lot."

"I thought Valerie and Rachel were friends of yours," said Kristy.

"I thought so, too," I said.

"That is *so mean!*" cried Mary Anne. "Why would Nan White start something like that? Well, actually I can see why *she* would do that, but why would Valerie and Rachel join in and laugh and stuff?"

"I don't know," I replied. "I'm glad they're not close friends. If they were, I'd feel like a real outcast. Instead I just feel . . . hurt, I guess."

"You have every right to feel hurt," spoke up Jessi. "They were being cruel."

"I wonder why some kids always want to hurt other kids," I mused.

"I don't know," said Jessi slowly. "I guess Nan was just born that way."

"Maybe," said Mary Anne thoughtfully, "Valerie and everybody were laughing because they're afraid. You know how sometimes you tease people because you need to feel that you're better than they are? Not that *you* tease, Mal. I mean, just in general. Well, maybe those girls were laughing to cover up the fact that *they're* afraid *their* parents might get fired someday. And they're glad it hasn't happened yet."

"Maybe," I answered. It was a good theory, but I didn't feel any better.

"Well," said Stacey, "don't worry, Mal. *We'll* stick by you."

"Definitely," agreed Claud.

"Right," added Jessi. "You all stuck by me when I first moved here and people snubbed me. Now we'll stick by you."

"The members of the BSC *always* stick together," said Kristy from the director's chair.

"I wish Jessi and I were in your grade," I told her. "Then we could really stick together."

"Boy, I'd like to teach Nan White something," said Kristy. "And Janet and Valerie and Rachel, too."

"Don't get carried away," Mary Anne warned her.

"I won't," Kristy promised.

"You guys are great," I said huskily.

"Oh, please. Don't start crying!" exclaimed Mary Anne.

And then we laughed again. We sounded like a rerun of the beginning of the meeting. But I couldn't help adding, just as Claud's clock turned to 6:00, "You're the best friends ever."

And Dawn said, "You'll get through this, Mal. I know you will."

I rode home that evening thinking that she was right, but not knowing just *how* I would get through it.

CHAPTER 6

"Smell this."

"Do I have to?"

"Yes. Just smell it."

"Ew. That is so gross. What is it?"

"My gym socks. Can't you tell?"

"No. They look like — "

"Don't listen to them, Mal!" Kristy hissed in my ear.

It was Monday, the afternoon of my first sitting job at the Delaneys'. Kristy and I were riding her bus home, and behind us, two kids were having a dibbly disgusting conversation, which was hard not to overhear.

"Concentrate on Amanda and Max," said Kristy. "I've got to give you some sitting tips on them, anyway, since this will be your first job with them."

"Okay," I replied.

"Now," began Kristy, "this is very important. *Don't let them get away with anything.*"

"Like what?" I asked.

"Anything they shouldn't be doing, or anything they *should* be doing for themselves. They love to test new sitters. Don't let them order you around."

"Kristy — " I interrupted.

"No, I'm serious. I know you're a good sitter, and I know you know how to control children, but Amanda and Max are a little bit different."

"Okay," I said uncertainly. I'd never met a kid I couldn't handle. However, I'd also never been given such a warning about sitting charges.

"Call me if you have any trouble," was the last thing Kristy said to me as we got off the bus. (The two kids who'd been sitting behind us were still talking about the smell of the decaying gym socks, trying to come up with an exact description of their odor. I was glad to leave them behind.)

"I will," I called to Kristy, even though I wouldn't. "Thanks for letting me ride with you!"

"You're welcome. . . . Good luck with Amanda and Max!"

Kristy crossed the street to her house and I walked slowly up the Delaneys' driveway.

Good luck? Would I really need luck that afternoon?

I hesitated on the Delaneys' front porch, then rang the bell. In a few moments, the door was opened by a tall woman who gave me a smile.

"Mallory?" she said.

"Yes. Mrs. Delaney?"

"Yup. Come on inside."

Now, I should stop here and tell you that from the outside, the Delaneys' house looked like any other mansion in the neighborhood. But inside! The inside of Kristy's house is like the inside of any house, only bigger. There are a lot of regular-looking rooms with toys and homework papers and jackets and sneakers scattered around. Inside the Delaneys' house was another story.

The first thing I saw, right in the front hall, was a *fountain*. Honest. A fountain that was *indoors*. It was golden, and in the shape of a fish standing on its tail. The water splashed out of its mouth and down into this pool that surrounded it.

Whoa.

I looked from left to right as Mrs. Delaney led me down a short hallway to the kitchen. We passed a library and a den and the living room. Oriental carpets and gilt-framed pictures were everywhere. And I didn't see a single speck of dust or anything on the floor that didn't belong there. Amanda and Max probably weren't allowed in those rooms. If they were, they must be pathologically neat, I thought. At the end of the hallway was the kitchen, which Kristy had told me looked like a space control center. She was right. It was full of gadgets and appliances, all gleaming white, that were operated mostly by button panels that looked as if they would light up when you touched them. I hoped I wouldn't have to use any of the gadgets to fix the kids an after-school snack. I'd be lucky to find the refrigerator.

"Okay," began Mrs. Delaney. "Amanda and Max should be home from school any minute now. Their bus gets here a little later than yours does. The emergency numbers are by the telephone. Our pediatrician is Doctor Evans. And our next-door neighbors are the Kilbournes — I think you know Shannon?" (I nodded.) "And the Winslows. . . . Let's see. Did Kristy tell you about our swimming pool?"

"No," I replied. How could Kristy have forgotten to mention that? I knew the Delaneys had two tennis courts, but I didn't know they had a pool.

"Okay," said Mrs. Delaney. "The pool was just installed. It's built in, of course." (Of *course*, I thought.) "Amanda and Max are both good swimmers. They can use the pool any time they want, as long as an adult is supervising them. When a sitter is in charge, then one of the next-door neighbors must be at home — just in case of an emergency. Both Mr. and Mrs. Kilbourne work, as you probably know, but Mrs. Winslow said she'd be home all afternoon, so swimming is okay today. Now, a lot of Amanda's and Max's friends want to go swimming as well. The rule for them is that when a sitter is in charge, they can only use the pool if they are good swimmers — if they can swim the width of the pool without stopping to rest. Amanda knows who those children are, and that the others may not go in the water."

"Okay," I said. "And I'm a good swimmer myself, so you don't need to worry."

Mrs. Delaney smiled, checked her watch, and announced, "Well, I'm off. I'll be back by five. Call Mrs. Winslow if you need her."

I breathed a sigh of relief as Mrs. Delaney pulled out of the driveway. Then I rummaged around the kitchen, found some fruit and graham crackers and set them on the table for Amanda and Max. A few moments later, I heard the front door open.

"Hello!" I called, running into the hallway.

There were Amanda and Max, storybook children in tidy school uniforms.

"Are you Mallory?" asked Amanda.

"Yup," I replied. "Hi, you guys. Your mom just left. She'll be back at five. I've got a snack ready for you in the kitchen."

"In the *kitch*en?!" exclaimed Amanda. "We never eat in there."

"Well, you're eating there today," I replied.

Amanda and Max didn't answer. They just set their school bags in the closet and followed me to the kitchen.

"Is that our snack?" asked Max, looking at the fruit and graham crackers in dismay. He eyed his sister.

"We always have Coke and Oreos — or whatever we want — for a snack," Amanda informed me, busily putting away the things I had set out.

I let the kids get away with this, since they had agreed to eat in the kitchen. Besides, I hadn't seen an Oreo or a bottle of Coke in several days.

The three of us sat down at the table, Max and Amanda looking at me curiously.

"Are you a friend of Kristy's?" asked Max.

"Yup," I replied. "I know her whole family. I know Shannon Kilbourne, too." (Shannon often baby-sits for the Delaneys.)

"Where do you live?" asked Amanda.

"On Slate Street."

Amanda frowned. "I don't know where that is. Which school do you go to — Stoneybrook Academy or Stoneybrook Day School?"

"Silly," said Max. "She must go to Stoneybrook Academy. *We* go to the day school, and we'd know if Mallory went there, too."

I smiled. "Actually, I go to Stoneybrook Middle School."

"Do you have any pets?" asked Max.

"Just a hamster. We used to have a cat, though."

"We have a cat," said Amanda. "Her name is Priscilla. She's a snow-white Persian and she cost four hundred dollars."

Four hundred dollars for a cat? I thought. Boy, you could get one free at a shelter. And you could certainly spend four hundred dollars on better things, like groceries.

"How about brothers and sisters?" asked Amanda.

"I've got seven," I said.

"*Seven!*" squealed Amanda. "Gosh, your father must be rich. What does he do? I bet it's something really important."

I believe it is always best to be honest with children, so I said, "Actually, my dad isn't working right now. He just lost his job."

"He did?" exclaimed Max.

"Well, *our* father," said Amanda, "is a partner in a *law firm*. He makes a lot of money. He gets Max and me whatever we want."

"Yeah," said Max. "We have tennis courts *and* a pool."

And a four-hundred-dollar cat, I thought. But all I said was, "I know."

"Our swimming pool is huge," said Amanda. "It has very beautiful steps in two corners and it's painted aquamarine blue and it has a slide and a diving board. Max and I go swimming all the time. Our friends come over to swim, too. We have lots of friends. Is Mrs. Winslow home, Mallory?"

"Yes," I answered.

"Goody."

The next thing I knew, Amanda was on the phone, inviting her friends to come to her house for a swim. Then she and Max changed into their bathing suits and ran outside. They jumped into the pool.

Of course, *I* didn't have *my* suit with me. So I sat in a lawn chair by the side of the pool and felt like a real dork.

Soon kids began to appear at the gate in the fence that surrounded the pool. The first three must have been the kids Amanda had phoned. She ran to the gate and let each of them in gleefully. I tried to watch five bouncy children and it wasn't easy, so I was alarmed when yet another kid, a girl about Max's age, came to the gate. But I felt relieved when Amanda stalked over to the girl and bossily said, "You can't come in. You can't swim yet."

My relief faded quickly when I saw the look on the girl's face, though. Chastised, she turned and walked slowly toward the driveway. Amanda watched her, looking smug.

Ten minutes later, the same thing happened with a little boy.

"Amanda!" I called.

Amanda trotted over to me. "Yeah?"

"Can't you tell them *nicely* that they can't swim today? I think you hurt that boy's feelings."

"Well, he deserved it. He hurt mine once. Besides, he can't swim."

"Amanda, don't use the pool as a way to get back at people. Or to make friends. I think you'll be sorry."

"Huh?" replied Amanda. She wasn't even listening. She was watching Max swoop down the slide and into the water with a splash.

"Never mind," I said, and Amanda ran off.

For the next hour I sat in the hot sun in my school clothes while the Delaneys and their friends played with their new toy. I thought of Claire at home who wanted a new toy, too — a Skipper doll she had seen advertised on TV. She knew she couldn't have it. Not now.

How unfair, I thought, as I looked around at the pool and the tennis courts and the big house with its fish fountain.

I felt like I was a nothing.

CHAPTER 7

Saturday

I sat at the Delaneys' house today. The weather was gorgeous, and the kids were already in the pool when I arrived— Amanda, Max, Karen Brewer, Timmy Hsu, and two kids I'd never met before whose names are Angie and Huck. (Huck isn't his real name, but that's what everyone calls him.)

Anyway, I see a little problem with Amanda and Max and the pool. You wrote about it after your first job at the Delaneys', Mal, but today it's taken a different course. This time, Amanda's feelings were hurt....

Stacey had gone on an unexpected Saturday job at the Delaneys'. Of course, the members of the BSC had offered it to me first, but I couldn't take it. I was just too busy. I was baby-sitting more than ever, and I felt pressured to do better than usual in school. I was going to need good grades to get a scholarship to college if Dad didn't find another job. Oh, sure, college was seven years away, but you just never know. It's always best to be prepared. Thrifty, too. I had learned a lot over the last week or so.

Anyway, that Saturday I was sitting for the Barretts for a couple of hours, and then I needed time to work on a social studies project. So Stacey went to the Delaneys'. She brought her bathing suit along, having learned from my first experience there. She didn't want to be unprepared.

Stacey has baby-sat for Amanda and Max before. They think she's weird. That's because when the BSC first began sitting for the Delaneys, and the kids were so awful, Stacey decided to use backwards psychology (or something like that) on Amanda and Max. When they became too demanding, she would encourage them to be more demanding (which caused them to behave). When they didn't want to clean up their playroom, Stacey made it into a huge mess — which the kids quickly cleaned up before their mother got home.

So Stacey could handle the Delaneys, but the kids thought she was a nut case.

As Stacey had written in the notebook, she arrived at Amanda and Max's to find them in the pool with four friends, one of whom (Karen Brewer) is Kristy's little stepsister. Mrs. Delaney had led Stacey out to the pool area (after Stace had changed into her bikini) and announced, "Kids, Stacey's here! She's in charge until your father and I get back. Remember the pool rules!"

"Okay, we will. 'Bye, Mommy!" Amanda called. (Max was underwater.)

Stacey seated herself at the edge of the shallow end of the pool, where most of the kids were playing. She let her legs dangle in the water.

"Hi, Stacey!" called Karen, who knows Stacey well. "Watch this!"

Karen scrambled out of the pool, backed up several paces, held her arms up in front of her, and said, "Okay, here I am, walking along, reading my newspaper. I'm just walking along — " SPLASH! Karen pretended to fall into the pool accidentally. The other kids laughed.

Amanda eyed Stacey. "Can I have a snack?" she asked.

Stacey sensed a test. She checked her watch. "It's two o'clock," she said. "Didn't you just have lunch?"

"Yes," admitted Amanda, "but I'm hungry again. I want — "

"Gosh, if you're hungry," said Stacey, "I better fix you a nice, healthy meal. That's the best way to make hunger go away. I'll get you some yogurt, some fruit, and maybe a small green salad."

"Oh, never mind," said Amanda. She pushed herself away from the edge of the pool, glided over to Max, and said to him (not very softly), "She's crazy. She is *so weird*."

"I know," replied Max, but he seemed unfazed. He was diving for a penny that he'd dropped on the floor of the pool.

Amanda and Karen played together for awhile. Angie practiced diving off the board into the deep end. And Timmy and Huck took one joyous ride after another down the slide and into the water. Presently, Amanda swam over to Stacey again, climbed out of the pool, and sat down next to her. Stacey placed a towel around her shoulders and patted her back.

"Thanks," said Amanda. She looked

thoughtful. Finally she said, "Do you know Mallory Pike? Our new baby-sitter?"

"Sure," replied Stacey.

"Her father . . . got *fired*."

"I know." Stacey wondered where this conversation was going and decided to let Amanda make the next move.

"What does your father do?" asked Amanda.

"He works for a company . . . in New York."

"In New *York?* Does he live there?"

"Yes," replied Stacey. "My parents are divorced."

Amanda frowned.

"But I get to visit my dad in the city whenever I want to."

"Really?" Amanda was impressed. "Does your father make a lot of money?"

Stacey was insulted. But she tried not to show it, even though she wanted desperately to say, "He makes enough to buy a four-hundred-dollar cat." Before she could come up with a polite answer, however, she was interrupted by Max.

He was climbing out of the pool, penny in hand.

"Stacey?" he said. "I'm tired of swimming."

"Me, too," said Amanda, who did not seem inclined to return to the water. "Max and I have been swimming all morning."

"Okay," Stacey answered. "Call your friends out of the pool and we'll find something else to do. Maybe we can play a game."

"Hey, you guys!" called Amanda, standing up. "It's time to get out of the pool. We're going to play a game."

"I don't want to get out," replied Huck immediately.

"Me, neither," said Angie. "I've got to practice my diving."

"Come on, Timmy!" called Max.

"No. I just got here."

"*Angie!*" Amanda whined.

"I'm diving," was the reply.

"I'll play with you, Amanda," said Karen, hoisting herself onto the side of the pool.

"Thanks," Amanda answered. Then she looked from the kids in the pool to Stacey. What was Stacey going to do about the situation? she seemed to be asking.

Clearly, Stacey had to do something. There was only one Stacey. She couldn't watch Timmy, Angie, and Huck in the pool, and Amanda, Karen, and Max somewhere else.

So Stacey stood up, too. "Okay, everybody out of the water!" she announced.

"I don't *want* to get out!" said Huck vehemently.

"And I have to practice," added Angie.

"I thought you guys came over to play with

Max and me," said Amanda, looking wounded. Her lower lip trembled ever so slightly.

"Well . . . well . . ." began Angie.

And Timmy said, "It's so hot today."

Max had said little until this point. Now he said, sounding almost afraid, "Huck? *Didn't* you come over to play with me?"

"I — " began Huck. He paused. Then he said, "Yeah. You and your pool."

"You guys are jerks!" Amanda shouted suddenly.

"No, we aren't. You are!" Angie retorted.

"Jerk, jerk, jerk!" chanted Max.

Timmy looked haughty. "I'm rubber, you're glue, and whatever you say bounces off me and sticks to you. So *you're* the jerk, Max."

"Okay, okay, okay," said Stacey firmly. "Enough. I'm in charge here. And I'm mostly in charge of Amanda and Max, and they don't want to play in the pool anymore. So, everybody out!"

Heaving great, exaggerated sighs, Huck, Angie, and Timmy got out of the pool. Max and Amanda brightened.

"Let's play dress-ups," Amanda said to Angie and Karen.

"Let's play dinosaurs," Max said to Huck and Timmy.

But Huck and Timmy were heading for the gate in the fence. "No, thanks," said Huck.

And Angie was gathering up her towel and a sundress. "I'm going to the Millers'," she informed everyone. "I'll practice in *their* pool."

Huck, Timmy, and Angie left.

Stacey looked at the distraught, confused faces of Max and Amanda. She wasn't sure what to say to them. So she was relieved when Karen spoke up.

"Do you have any new dress-up clothes?" Karen asked Amanda. Then she added, "It doesn't matter if you do or not. You know what? We haven't played Lovely Ladies in a long time. Do you still have your Lovely Ladies clothes?"

Amanda nodded, trying not to cry.

"Well, then," said Stacey brightly, "why don't you two go upstairs, take off your wet suits, and turn yourselves into Lovely Ladies? Max, what do you want to do? You could invite another friend over."

Max shook his head. He and Stacey were following the girls into the house.

"Would you like me to read to you?" Stacey asked him.

"I guess." Max shrugged.

"Okay." Stacey waited for Max to get dressed. Then she settled down with him in the Delaneys' immaculate white playroom and read him book after book. Max only half listened to the stories.

And from the sounds of things in Amanda's room, the game of Lovely Ladies was only halfhearted.

CHAPTER 8

At home, our days fell into a pattern that was different from (but also similar to) the one we had had before Dad lost his job. Our family continued to get up at six-thirty in the morning on weekdays. My brothers and sisters and I got up then so we would arrive at school on time. Mom got up then so she would be ready if the agency called and said she had a job somewhere that day. And Dad got up then in case Mom *did* have a job. Then he would help fix breakfast and get us kids off to school.

When we came home in the afternoon, Dad would be looking for a job. He spent a lot of time poring over the want ads in the paper and even more time on the phone. I looked at the want-ads section once after Dad had been through it. Some of the little boxes were circled in pencil, some were circled vigorously in ink, and others had been circled with a red

71

felt-tip pen. Phone numbers and names were scribbled all up and down the margins of the pages.

Claire complained, "Daddy never plays with me after he picks me up from school. He just sits in the kitchen and works."

"He's trying to find another job," I told her. "That's very important, remember? He needs a job so he can earn money again."

"So I can get the Skipper doll?"

"So you can get the Skipper doll."

Meanwhile, Mom had gone out on pretty many jobs. I couldn't tell if she liked what she was doing or not. Most of the jobs were secretarial. Mom said she would type letters for people and file papers and answer telephones. She made the work sound boring, but to me, it sounded better than changing sheets and ironing clothes at home, although not better than the volunteer work my mother does. Mom said she liked word processing, though. She likes computers, which I hadn't expected, and seems to know a lot about them, which I also hadn't expected.

After about two weeks of this routine, things changed slightly. Mom was working three or four days a week. But Dad seemed to have slowed down his job hunt.

"Why?" I asked him.

"Because I've exhausted most of the possibilities," he replied. "I'm beginning to see the same jobs listed over and over in the paper. I've sent out copies of my résumé, I've made phone calls. Now there's nothing left to do except wait for people to call and say they want to arrange interviews."

Dad looked discouraged — and right when I thought he should be feeling good. He'd done all the hard work. Now he just had to sit back and wait for the phone to ring.

One Tuesday, not long after Dad said he'd "exhausted the possibilities," I came home from school earlier than usual. I had no sitting job that afternoon, and school had come to an abrupt end ten minutes before the final bell because we'd had a false fire alarm. I parked my bike in our garage and ran inside, expecting to find Dad in the kitchen with the paper.

Instead, I found him sprawled in an easy chair in the rec room. He was wearing blue jeans, a T-shirt, and these awful old slippers that the triplets tease him about. Next to him was a box of crackers, half empty, and in his hand was a glass of something. The TV was playing — a game show was on, I think — but Dad didn't seem to be paying attention to it. His eyes were aimed in the direction of the TV set, but I could tell he was not trying to come up with the answer to the clue "favorite clothing of idiots." (The answer was "dunce caps.")

And I hoped he hadn't been watching TV all day. He would make our electricity bill too high.

"Dad?" I said. "Where's Claire?"

"Huh?" I realized that although I had not been quiet about coming home, Dad hadn't been aware of my presence until I spoke. "Oh, hi, Mal," he said absently.

"Hi. Where's Claire?" I repeated.

"Claire? She was here awhile ago." Dad glanced around the room until his eyes settled on the TV screen again.

"Claire? Claire!" I called. I dropped my books on the floor and ran upstairs to the kitchen. On the way, I imagined two things. 1. Claire was missing. 2. Claire had taken advantage of things and made a huge mess somewhere. I decided the second possibility was more likely. But I was wrong. Claire was neither missing nor a mess. She was sitting on her bed in the room she shares with Margo, playing with two old baby dolls.

"Bad!" she was saying to one of the dolls. "Bad girl. You put that back. You can't have it. Daddy is fired now."

She turned to the other doll. "Stop it!" she

cried. "Quit pestering me. I just told you —
you *can't* have a new Skipper. And that's
final!"

"Hi, Claire," I said.

Claire dropped the dolls and glanced up,
looking somewhat guilty. "Hi," she replied.

"Have you been playing up here all afternoon?" I asked her.

"Pretty much," said Claire. "I went downstairs three times to ask Daddy to play with
me, and he just said, 'Not now.' "

"Did Daddy give you lunch after school?"

"He said I could have whatever I wanted."

"What did you want?"

"Twinkies, but we didn't have any." Claire's
chin was trembling.

"So you didn't eat?"

Claire shook her head. "Daddy is an old
silly-billy-goo-goo."

I sat down on the bed and put my arms
around my sister.

I don't know for sure what Dad did the next
afternoon, because it was Wednesday and I
sat at the Delaneys' and then went to Claudia's
for the BSC meeting. I think Dad did pretty
much the same things as he had the day before, though. At any rate, when I came home
from the meeting, he was wearing the T-shirt,

jeans, and decrepit slippers again. But at least he was in the kitchen helping Mom fix dinner.

On Thursday afternoon, I came home loaded with schoolwork. My social studies teacher had assigned another project, I had a French test coming up, and both my math and science teachers had given us more homework than usual. Ordinarily, I would just have done the best I could in whatever amount of time I had. But now I was determined to get straight A's. (I'd need them for that college scholarship.) So I planned to shut myself up in my bedroom and study until bedtime, taking time out for dinner only.

But Dad ruined my plans.

After school, I found him once again parked in front of the TV, wasting electricity, this time wearing his bathrobe and pajamas. And the slippers, of course. A soap opera was on TV. Dad has always said soap operas are silly, but he seemed sort of interested in this one.

"Hi, Dad," I said wearily. "Where are Claire and Margo and Nicky?" (Mom was working that day. I knew Margo and Nicky had gotten home from school because their bikes were parked in the garage.)

"Upstairs," replied Dad vaguely.

"Dad? Are you okay?" I asked. I had been angry with him on Tuesday. Today I was worried. Maybe he was sick. Maybe that was why he was in his bathrobe and pajamas.

"I'm fine," Dad answered, not taking his eyes off the television.

"Are you sure?"

Dad came to life. "I'm *sure.* I just wish everyone would quit asking how I am and leave me alone."

"Okay, okay, okay," I said. I figured that Margo, Nicky, and Claire had asked him the same thing and been yelled at, too. Then it dawned on me. Claire. If Dad was still in his pajamas, and Mom was at work, how had Claire gotten home from kindergarten? Had Dad gone out in public in his pajamas? Had he let Claire *walk* home from school? She'd never done that before.

"Claire? Claire?" I shouted. I bounded upstairs. I did not need this problem today. Not before my French test on a night when I had at least two nights' worth of studying to do.

"Yeah?" Claire replied.

She and Margo and Nicky were in the living room, sitting in a row on the couch. They looked like they were in a doctor's waiting room.

"What's going on, you guys?" I asked. Then, before I gave them a chance to answer, I said, "Claire, how did you get home from school today?"

"Myriah's mommy picked me up."

"Mrs. Perkins? Why did she pick you up?"

"Because Daddy called her and asked her to."

I didn't pursue the subject. It would have to wait until Mom came home. "So what *are* you guys doing here?"

Margo and Nicky glanced at each other. "Daddy yelled at us," said Margo.

"Did he tell you to come up here and sit on the couch?" I wanted to know.

Nicky shook his head. "Nope. We just felt like being together."

"And Daddy said, *'Leave me alone!'* " added Claire.

Great, I thought. Dad wasn't going to watch the kids. So I would have to. But how would I study? In the end, I encouraged Margo and Nicky to go to friends' houses, and the triplets to play baseball in the backyard. Then I parted with some of my hard-earned baby-sitting money to pay Vanessa to watch Claire.

When Mom came home late that afternoon, she was not happy to hear about any of this — particularly the part about Dad asking Mrs. Perkins to bring Claire home from kindergarten.

She confronted Dad in the rec room, where he had become, I decided, an official couch potato. "This is — " she started to say loudly.

Then she seemed to change her mind. She also lowered her voice. "I cannot," she said, "work all day, come home, make dinner, *clean up the house*," (I looked around and saw that the rec room had become a wreck room) "*and* help the children with their homework."

"Mom," I said, feeling guilty, "I'm sorry about the house. I should have cleaned it up this afternoon, but I — "

"It's not your fault," my mother interrupted me. "And it's not your job, either. You have homework and baby-sitting." She turned to Dad. "It's *your* job," she said flatly. "When I go to work and you stay at home, then you keep house, just like I do when I'm at home."

"Ex*cuse* me?" replied my father.

A fight was coming on. I could tell. I glanced up at the stairs, saw my brothers and sisters huddled in the kitchen, watching, and led them to their rooms.

We couldn't overhear the fight — it wasn't loud enough — but my mother must have won. By the following Tuesday, Dad had taken over Mom's old role completely. He wasn't much of a cook, but dinner was ready when I came home from the Friday and Monday BSC meetings. The house grew neater and cleaner — and so did Dad. He started getting dressed again.

And on that Tuesday, when I returned from

school, loaded with homework again, I found Dad and Claire together in the kitchen, working on a project together. Dad was up to his elbows in Elmer's glue and macaroni.

For some reason, that scene scared me more than the couch-potato scene had. That night, I called another meeting of the Pike Club.

CHAPTER 9

It took me awhile to realize why the sight of Dad and Claire had scared me. I should have been dibbly happy to see my father so cheerful. And wearing shoes. I should have been happy to find a neat house, clean bathrooms, and spaghetti sauce simmering on the stove. I should have been happy that Dad had picked up Claire from school himself and had thought of an afternoon art activity for her. But I wasn't.

Why? Because, I realized after almost twenty minutes of thinking when I should have been doing my homework, Dad looked like he was enjoying himself. What if he didn't find another job? What if he didn't *care* that he didn't find another job?

That was only one reason why I called the meeting of the Pike Club.

The triplets, Vanessa, Nicky, Margo, Claire, and I gathered, once again, in my bedroom.

Nobody else was as worried as I was. My brothers and sisters liked the club meetings, so they didn't care why I had called one.

"So," I began, when we had all settled down, and Nicky had stopped pulling Margo's hair, "how are you guys doing?"

"I still want Skipper," said Claire immediately.

"I know you do," I told her. "Skipper will have to wait, though."

"Yeah. Silly-billy-goo-goo." (Claire is not known for being patient.)

Nobody else said anything, but the triplets looked uncomfortable.

"School going okay?" I asked.

The boys looked, if possible, even more uncomfortable.

"You know what's happening to *me* in school?" I said.

"What?" asked Byron with considerable interest.

"These girls are teasing me about Dad. Nan White and Janet O'Neal started it. They're awful anyway. But then Valerie and Rachel joined them. Nan passed around this note in the cafeteria — I found the note later, I think Nan *wanted* me to find it — and Janet and Valerie and Rachel were all laughing like crazy."

"Valerie?" spoke up Adam. "Wasn't she the

one who used to come home from school with you sometimes last year?"

"Yup," I replied. "And Rachel and I were science partners in fifth grade. We always had fun together."

"What did Nan's note say?" asked Vanessa.

"It said, 'Mallory's going to be on welfare,' " I replied. "First of all, that's not true," (I hope, I thought) "and secondly, if it were true, it's not something to tease about. Besides, a lot of people go on welfare."

Claire opened her mouth then and I *knew* she was going to ask what welfare was, so I was relieved when Jordan started speaking before she could.

"Michael Hofmeister won't play ball with Byron and Adam and me anymore," he said, looking at his brothers.

"How come?" I asked, frowning.

"We aren't sure," said Byron. "One day he was teasing us because we couldn't bring in money to go on a field trip with our after-school baseball team, and the next day we asked him over and he said no and we've asked him two *more* times and he still says no."

"People can be pretty mean," I said. (Byron looked like he wanted to cry.)

"But some people are nice," said Vanessa,

which, fortunately, saved Byron from crying.

"Oh, yeah?" I replied. "Who?"

"Becca Ramsey. She gave me fifty cents yesterday when I wanted a Popsicle really, really badly."

"Well, that *is* nice," I said, smiling.

"Boy, I'd like to *get* Michael Hofmeister," said Jordan.

"Me, too," said Adam. "I'd like to open his lunch one day and put crushed-up spiders in his peanut butter sandwich."

"Ew, gross!" squealed Margo.

"I'd like to accidentally hit him in the head with a baseball," said Jordan.

"Jordan!" I cried.

"*I'd* like to get *his* father fired from *his* job and *then* Michael would see how it feels," exclaimed Byron. "And I'd laugh at *him* when *he* couldn't go on a field trip."

"I," said Vanessa to me, "wish you would write mean notes about Valerie and Rachel, but especially about Nan White and Janet O'Neal, and put the notes up all over school where everyone could read them."

"Okay, you guys. Enough," I said gently. "We have other things to discuss."

"What other things?" asked Nicky.

"Money," I replied.

"Money? Again? That's all we ever talk about," complained Margo. "We've been

84

trying and trying to save money."

"I know. And you've been doing a great job," I told her. "But now we need to figure out some ways to *earn* money."

"How come?" asked Claire.

"Because Dad isn't earning any money now, and Mom is earning some, but it isn't even *close* to what Dad used to earn. I bet that maybe — *maybe* — it pays for food each week. And necessities."

"What are nessities?" Claire wanted to know.

"Ne*cess*ities, dumbbell," Adam replied. "They're things you really need, like soap and toothpaste and toilet paper."

"Toilet paper!" hooted Claire. (You just never know what will make her laugh.)

"Anyway," I went on, "so Mom's probably paying for food and stuff, but we *still* have to pay the mortgage — " I glanced at Claire.

She was looking at me. "I'm sorry," she said. "I don't know what a mortgage is, either. I can't help it."

"That's all right," I told her. (I was betting that most of my brothers and sisters didn't know what a mortgage is, any more than Claire did.) I tried to think how to explain that term. "See," I began. "We don't own our house ourselves yet. The bank owns part of it."

"The bank?" Nicky asked. "Which part does the bank own?"

I sighed. "No particular part. It's just that when Mom and Dad bought our house, they didn't have enough money to pay for the whole thing. So they borrowed money from the bank. Most people do that. Now we have to pay the bank back, a little each month. Well, not a *little* — I don't know how much exactly. Plus, we have to pay the electricity bill, the phone bill, and the gas bill. And all those bills are high since there are ten people in our family. So I bet Mom and Dad are using the money in our savings account already. I just keep wondering: When the money in our savings account is gone, what will happen to our family? What will we do?"

Byron looked concerned. Then he said, "Dad'll probably have a job before we run out of money."

"Maybe. But maybe not," I countered. "I think we should be prepared."

"How?" asked Vanessa and Margo at the same time.

"Well, we could earn money to put in the savings account. I've been hoarding all my baby-sitting money since Dad lost his job. I'll give it to Mom and Dad soon."

"We could earn money, too!" Jordan cried.

(I'd been hoping someone would say that.)

"Yeah!" said Vanessa, inspired, "and I know exactly what I could do."

"What?" I asked, feeling suspicious, but I wasn't sure why.

"I could sell my poems to magazines!"

Vanessa is an aspiring poet. She has notebooks and notebooks filled with her poetry. Sometimes she even speaks in rhyme, which is annoying.

"Vanessa — " I started to say. (The triplets were snickering.)

"No, really. I could," said Vanessa. "Don't laugh."

Of course, Adam laughed even harder. Then he added, "Don't worry. We're not laughing at you . . . we're just laughing near you."

Vanessa smiled at that. Then she said, "I really am going to try it, though. Writing poetry is what I do best."

"Hey!" cried Margo. "You know what I saw in a magazine the other day? Wait a sec. I'll go get it."

"I bet she saw one of those ads to draw 'Blinkie' or whatever it is," said Jordan. "Now she thinks she can become a famous artist."

But what Margo returned with was a page from some magazine that said: *If y cn rd ths, y cn bcm a secy and gt a gd jb.*

"That says," Margo began proudly, " 'If you

can read this, you can become a secretary and get a good job.' Well, I can read it, and I'm only seven. So I can *certainly* get a good job."

"As an after-school secretary?" said Byron, teasing.

"Well, you never know. Maybe I could sign up at that temporary place where Mommy works."

"Margo, I'm not sure about that," I said.

"Me, neither," added Jordan. "I'm going to do something I know will work. I'm going to mow people's lawns."

"I could pet-sit, or walk people's dogs," said Byron.

"Maybe I'll, um, I'll . . ." Adam trailed off.

"Wait! I know!" cried Byron. "The three of us could start an odd-job service. We'll call it ABJ, Incorporated."

"ABJ?" I repeated.

"Yeah. Adam, Byron, Jordan."

"Now I *like* that idea," I said. "That's using your heads, you guys."

"Maybe I could get a paper route," said Nicky thoughtfully.

Before one of the triplets could jump down his throat I said, "Another good idea, Nick-o. Why don't you see if any of your friends has a paper route? Find out what you have to do to get one."

"Okay." Nicky grinned.

At this point, Margo lost her head for a moment and thought she was in school. She raised her hand.

"Margo?" I said, over the giggles of the other kids.

"If an after-school secretary isn't a good job, then maybe I could set up a lemonade stand. Claire, you could help me. Vanessa, too. *We* could be CMV, Incorporated."

"I think you'll just have to be CM, Incorporated. I'm still going to work on my poetry," said Vanessa.

So the job problems were solved. But something was bothering Byron.

"Mal?" he said. "If we don't pay our mortgage, what happens?"

"I'm not sure," I replied honestly, "but I think that, after awhile, the bank can take our house away from us."

"And that," said Byron, "is probably how some people become homeless."

CHAPTER 10

Sunday

Today I baby-sat for Linny, Hannie, and Sari Papadakis. They're such nice kids. I'm really glad that Linny and David Michael are friends, and that Hannie and Karen are friends. Maybe someday Sari and Emily Michelle will be friends, too.

The morning started out cloudy and cool, so the Papadakis kids wanted to play inside. But they invited Karen and David Michael over. Everyone, including Sari, played well together — for once. (Usually the boys won't play with the girls.) But then the sun came out and things changed. Hanny and Linny's feelings got hurt, and guess who was responsible for that. My own brother and sister, that's who....

The Papadakis kids are favorite sitting charges of Kristy, in case you couldn't tell from her notebook entry. Linny is nine (a little older than David Michael), Hannie is seven and in the same class with Karen at their private school, and Sari is just two. They live on the other side of the street from Kristy, two houses away from the Delaneys. (Shannon Kilbourne lives between the Delaneys and the Papadakises.)

As Kristy wrote, that Sunday morning was cloudy and cool.

"Can we invite friends over?" Hannie asked Kristy as soon as her parents had left. She was looking forlornly out the window.

"Sure," replied Kristy. "Who do you want to invite?"

"Karen!" said Hannie.

"David Michael!" said Linny.

"Well, that's easy," Kristy told them, smiling. "They're home. And they're probably bored. Do you want me to call them?"

"Yes," said Linny seriously, nodding his head.

So Kristy called home and invited her brother and sister over.

"What shall we do?" asked Karen as soon as she and David Michael had stepped into the Papadakises' house.

"Let's play with Myrtle the turtle and Noodle the poodle," said David Michael.

"Nah. We already did that today," Linny told him.

"Dolls!" Karen suggested to Hannie.

"Nah," said Hannie.

"Invaders from the planet Neptune?" Linny suggested to David Michael.

"Nah," said David Michael.

"Hey!" cried Karen. "I know something we've never played, *and* we can all play it together. Even Sari. Even you, Kristy."

"What?" said the boys suspiciously. (Most of Karen's games involve either dolls, witches, or dressing up, none of which interests Linny or David Michael.)

"We can play office."

"Office?" repeated Hannie.

"Yes. We'll set up one of your desks like a desk in a real office — with papers and pencils and paper clips and — "

"And that old telephone that doesn't work," added Linny, getting into the spirit of things. "It'll be good because it's a *real* phone, not a plastic one."

Kristy couldn't believe that the four kids wanted to play together, but they were already racing upstairs. She followed, holding Sari's hand as Sari climbed the steps one at a time, one at a time.

The kids chose the desk in Hannie's room, and in no time it looked pretty officelike.

"Let's make a waiting area," suggested David Michael.

"Yeah," said Karen. "All offices have waiting rooms with magazines."

So Linny dragged a chair into his sister's room, placed it next to her chair, and put a small table in between them. Then Hannie ran downstairs and returned with a pile of magazines.

"I got some Golden Books, too," she said. "For Sari. In case she has to wait."

"Oh," said Kristy, "is this a doctor's office?"

Hannie, Linny, David Michael, and Karen looked at each other.

"I don't want to play doctor's office," said Linny. "That's for babies."

"Besides, we wouldn't need desks; we'd need tables and stethoscopes and those little hammers," said Karen sensibly.

"We'll play something really grown-up," said Linny, thinking hard. "We'll play . . . we'll play job agency."

"Job agency?" said Hannie, perplexed.

"Yeah. I saw it on *I Love Lucy* once. Lucy and Ethel needed jobs, so they went to this office and a man there said, 'What do you do?' and Lucy said, 'What kind of jobs do you have open?' and the man said, 'What do you do?'

and anyway, finally, Lucy and Ethel ended up working in a factory that makes chocolate candies.''

"Wow! Fun!" cried Karen.

"What parts are we going to play?" Kristy asked.

Not until after a lot of squabbling and arguing were the parts assigned. It was decided that Karen and Hannie would own the job agency. They would sit behind the desk. And Linny, David Michael, and Kristy would be people needing jobs. (Sari was going to play Kristy's daughter.)

"Okay," said Hannie. "Let's begin. Our office is open!"

"I'll be your first customer," said David Michael, "since I need a job really, really, really bad."

"Badly," Kristy corrected him absentmindedly. She was thinking of my father.

"Badly," David Michael repeated.

He stepped up to the desk. Linny, Kristy, and Sari sat in the "waiting room," Sari in Kristy's lap. Linny looked at a magazine. Kristy read a story to Sari.

Meanwhile, David Michael was saying, "Hello, my name is David Michael Thomas and I need a job. Really badly."

"Okay," said Karen. "What kind of work do you do?"

"What kind of jobs do you have open?"

"Well, what kind of work do you do?" asked Karen again.

"It depends. What kind of jobs do you have — have open?" David Michael got the giggles then, and so did the girls, then Linny, then Kristy, and then even Sari, although she didn't know what was going on.

When the giggling died down, Hannie said, "Let me look at my list of jobs. Okay." She pretended to scan a sheet of paper. (The paper was blank.) "We need a substitute teacher. Do you teach school?"

David Michael shook his head.

"Do you cook? A restaurant needs a chef."

"I can make toast," said David Michael. "And chocolate milk."

"You're hired!" cried Hannie.

"Oh, thank you, thank you," said David Michael. "Now I can feed my family again. And buy clothes for them."

The kids giggled, but Kristy found herself thinking about Dad and *my* family again. Would Dad be reduced to going to some agency and taking a job he was overqualified for? Would he end up as a waiter in a restaurant — when he had gone to school for his law degree?

Kristy told me later that she felt a lump in her stomach, just thinking about these things, and that she was relieved when, about an hour later, the sun came out and Linny cried, "Oh, good! We can go outdoors!"

The game of "job agency" was abandoned, and Kristy accompanied the five kids into the backyard.

"Hey, it's warm enough to go swimming," David Michael pronounced.

"Yeah!" said Karen. "Let's go over to Amanda and Max's."

"You're going to go over to Amanda's?" repeated Hannie in dismay. Amanda is slightly older than Karen, but the girls are friends anyway. Not best friends, but friends. Hannie, on the other hand, who lives in Amanda's neighborhood day in and day out (not just on the weekends like Karen), can't stand Amanda. The feeling is mutual. Amanda doesn't like Hannie much, either.

"Yes. Now it's a perfect day to go swimming," said Karen. "Come on, Hannie."

"No way," Hannie answered. "I don't like Amanda. You know that."

"But you want to go swimming, don't you?"

"Not badly enough to go over to the Delaneys'."

David Michael looked at Linny. "You'll go swimming, won't you?" he asked.

"No," answered Linny. "I don't like the Delaneys, either. And neither do *you*. How come you're going?"

"Because . . . I . . . want . . . to . . . go . . . swimming," said David Michael impatiently.

"Okay, go ahead," said Linny.

"Yeah, go ahead," Hannie said to Karen. "I don't care."

"Okay, we will," Karen replied haughtily.

"You guys," said Kristy warningly. "Is the pool worth fighting over?"

"We're not fighting," Karen told her.

Kristy could have guessed otherwise, as her brother and sister left, and Hannie and Linny remained behind. Hannie looked close to tears, but Linny just began to dismantle the "job agency." He was very quiet.

"That is so unfair," Hannie cried.

"I'm sorry they left," said Kristy.

"It's not just that," Hannie replied. "I know Karen wants to go swimming. And she and Amanda are friends. I wish Karen had stayed here, but I guess Karen has a right to play with other kids. But David Michael doesn't like the Delaneys at all. I think it's unfair of him to use their pool when he doesn't even *like* them. Amanda and Max probably think he wants to play with *them*."

"Yeah," Linny spoke up finally. (He was gathering together the mazagines and books.)

"I would never go somewhere just to use someone's pool. It really isn't fair. Hannie's right."

"Do a lot of kids use the Delaneys' pool?" asked Kristy.

"Oh, tons," Hannie answered. "Amanda and Max think they're the most popular kids in Stoneybrook." She sounded very wise.

"How many of these kids are really Amanda and Max's friends?" Kristy wanted to know.

"A few, I guess," said Linny.

"But the rest of the kids are taking advantage of the Delaneys?"

"Yup," replied Linny.

Hmm, thought Kristy. That was a problem. She'd seen it coming, but she didn't know just how bad it had gotten. Worse, her own brother and sister were part of the problem. At least, David Michael was. Karen truly is friends with Amanda, but she shouldn't have deserted Hannie that morning.

After Kristy left the Papadakises', she called to tell me what was going on.

CHAPTER 11

I was at the Delaneys' again. It was a Wednesday afternoon, one of my regular days there. And I was sitting at the edge of the pool in my bathing suit, sipping a Coke. Behind me was a mansion with a fish fountain inside. In front of me, beyond the pool, a green lawn rolled down to tennis courts.

I felt like a princess — except that I was a paid princess. This wasn't my mansion, my fountain, my pool, my lawn, or my tennis courts. And the four-hundred-dollar cat that was dozing on the sun-warmed pavement beside me wasn't mine, either.

But I could dream, couldn't I?

So I did dream as I watched Amanda, Max, Timmy, Angie, and Huck play in the water. Long before anything actually happened, though, I stopped my dreaming and started paying even closer attention to the children. I don't know why. I could just sense something brewing.

On the surface, everything seemed all right. Angie was practicing her diving, as usual. And she was doing nicely, jackknifing and tumbling off the board. The boys were taking turns whooshing down the slide into the water, calling out things like, "Bombs away!" and "Look out below!" And Amanda was floating around on a raft shaped like a turtle, her legs hanging over the end. She was reading *Superfudge*, by Judy Blume, and was lost in a world of her own.

What first made me pay even stricter attention to things, was Max's saying, "Let's be otters at the zoo instead of dive-bombers, okay? Then we can go down the slide on our stomachs."

Okay, so Max had gotten tired of dive-bombing.

Big deal.

Then Amanda closed *Superfudge* with a sigh and said, "What a great book."

"Are you finished with it?" I asked her.

"Yup. And I just began it yesterday." Amanda paddled herself to the side of the pool, handed me the book so that it wouldn't get wet, and then climbed out of the pool and sat next to me.

"Hey, Angie!" she called. "I finished *Super-*

fudge. Now will you play with me?"

Angie had just emerged from underwater. Her hair was slicked back from her face.

"I've got a diving meet next week," was her reply.

"So are you here to play with Amanda or to practice?" I couldn't help asking.

Amanda looked at me in awe. Then she sat up straight and said, "Yeah, are you here to play with me or to practice?"

Angie blushed to the roots of her hair. "Um — " she began, but she was interrupted by Max, who clearly had tired of the pool altogether. He was standing next to me, drying himself off.

"What's up, Max?" I asked.

"I want to go hit balls in the tennis court," he said.

"We don't!" Timmy said, apparently speaking for both himself and Huck.

"Bombs away!" added Huck as he catapulted into the water.

"How about you?" I asked Amanda gently. I sensed another scene coming on like the one Stacey had written about.

"I — I don't know," replied Amanda, not sounding at all like the self-important snob she'd been the first time I sat at the Delaneys'.

"Have you had enough swimming?"

Amanda nodded.

So I was faced with Stacey's problem. I was in charge at the Delaneys'. The Delaney kids did not want to swim. But there were three other kids in the pool. I had to do what Stacey had done.

"Okay! Angie! Huck! Timmy! Out of the pool! It's time to do something else. You can play tennis with Max or . . . or . . ."

Amanda tugged at my suit and I leaned down. She whispered in my ear.

"Or," I continued loudly, "Cabbage Patch dolls with Amanda."

These suggestions were met with groans.

"But I have a *new* doll," said Amanda.

"So what. So do I," said Angie.

"Well, you guys still have to get out of the pool," I said.

Angie, Huck, and Timmy did so, with much huffing, grumbling things like, "What a rip-off," and, "Thanks for nothing!"

Even so, Amanda and Max looked at me gratefully. Amanda went so far as to say, "Thank you, Mallory."

When Huck and Timmy and Angie had dried off, Max said, "Okay, I've got extra rackets for you guys."

And Amanda said, "My new doll is upstairs, Angie."

But Huck, Angie, and Timmy walked

straight through the gate in the fence surrounding the pool. They did this wordlessly.

Amanda looked at me with her mouth open, while Max just watched the other kids leave.

"I don't believe it!" Amanda exclaimed. "I *don't believe* it!" She sounded both angry and bewildered.

I put my arm around her. Then I put my arm around Max. "Come on. Let's sit down for a few minutes." I started to lead them over to some lawn chairs, but Max wriggled away.

"I'm still going to practice hitting balls," he said. And he disappeared into the house to change and to look for his tennis racket.

Amanda, however, stuck with me. She seemed to want to talk.

"How come Angie wouldn't play with me?" she asked. "I thought she was my friend." She paused. "Oops. Am I being bossy?"

Poor Amanda. She really can be bossy, and someone must have given her a hard time about it. Now she was sensitive to it.

"Not at all," I assured her. "If you were being bossy, you would have said, 'Angie, get out of the pool and play dolls with me!' "

"You said that!" Amanda told me, giggling.

"I guess I did," I replied. "Sort of."

Amanda's smile faded. "Then if I'm not being bossy, what's wrong? I mean, I want kids to come over here and play with me. And with Max. I don't want kids to play with the *pool*."

"I can understand that," I told her.

"You know what?" said Amanda.

"What?"

"I don't know if the kids like Max and me, or if they just like the pool. I really don't know." She was beginning to cry. "Are they our friends or not? Do they like me?"

I stroked Amanda's hair and let her cry. And all the while I was thinking, Maybe being a "princess" isn't so great. Would you always wonder whether people liked *you* or whether they liked the things you could do for them — like letting them swim in your pool or play with your fancy toys, or lending them money, or introducing them to other rich kids.

It was no picnic having an out-of-work father, but at least I knew where I stood with my friends. Obviously Jessi liked *me*. I certainly didn't have anything besides myself to offer her these days, and she had stuck around. Nothing had changed between us.

I ached for Amanda — and at the same time I coveted her pool and house and four-hundred-dollar cat.

I had also found out who my friends *weren't*.

"You know what?" I said to Amanda.

"What?" she asked.

"I learned some pretty important things when my dad lost his job."

"You did?"

"Yup. I saw who stuck by me and who didn't. The ones who stuck by me are my real friends. The others are . . ."

"Enemies?" suggested Amanda.

"No, not enemies. But people I can't trust. People who care more about what their friends have than about who their friends are."

"Oh."

"So I was thinking. Even though your family is pretty different from mine, you and I are having sort of the same problem. Now you've got a swimming pool and you don't know who to trust. Do your friends like you because of what you have or because of who you are?"

"I don't know," replied Amanda.

"I bet you could find out."

"Really? How?"

"Well," I began, "maybe you could tell Angie and Karen and whoever else has been swimming here that you're not allowed to have friends use the pool when a sitter is in charge. Tell them it's a new rule or something. Then see who will still come over to play."

Amanda wiped some tears away with the back of her hand. She actually smiled. "That's a good idea," she said.

"Thanks."

"And you know what else I'm going to do? I'm going to tell *off* the kids who *don't* come over to play! Mallory, I'm so glad you're my baby-sitter."

I guessed it no longer mattered to Amanda that Dad was out of a job. We were conspirators. We had a plan.

I just hoped that some kids *would* play with Amanda.

CHAPTER 12

That night, I felt inspired. I lay in bed unable to sleep because I was thinking about my conversation with Amanda. I decided to take my own advice. And some of Amanda's.

My room was dark, the shades drawn against the streetlights, but one of the windows was wide open, so I snuggled under the covers, listening to the nighttime sounds: the last crickets, a car turning into the driveway of the house across the street, my parents locking our front door before they went to bed. On the other side of the room, Vanessa tossed in her sleep and made funny noises with her mouth.

What I wanted to do was confront the kids who had been mean to me. But right away, I thought of two questions. Was it worth confronting them? After all, I had my BSC friends. And if I did decide to confront Valerie and the others, how would I do it? Would I just walk up to them and say, "You're not my friends anymore"? Would I say, "Friends don't treat friends this way"?

By the next morning I only had an answer to my first question. I had decided to confront my former friends. Maybe the BSC members had stuck by me, but not everyone had. Rachel and Valerie hadn't even *tried* to be understanding. They had just listened to Nan and Janet — and then they had snubbed me. They were prejudiced against me because my father had lost his job. It was the principle of the thing, and I wasn't going to let them get away with it. If nothing else, I needed to stand up for myself.

I just wasn't sure how.

So I talked to Jessi about it in the cafeteria that day. Jessi had bought the hot lunch, and I had brought lunch from home. Mom said it was cheaper to make sandwiches for us kids than to give us money. Of course, nothing very interesting went into our bag lunches — just sandwiches and fruit — but we didn't complain because we knew we were helping our parents out, and that was important.

Jessi and I sat down at the end of a long table in the cafeteria, separating ourselves from other kids. Jessi knew I wanted to talk privately.

I looked at the food in front of us: my peanut butter and jelly sandwich and apple, and Jessi's pizzaburger and limp salad.

"Gross me out," I said.

"I know," Jessi replied. "So what did you want to talk about?"

I glanced around the room. Valerie, Rachel, Nan, and Janet were sitting just one table away, so I leaned over and whispered to Jessi, "I want to get even with Valerie and everybody. Well, especially with Nan White and Janet O'Neal, since they started everything."

"How are you going to do it?" Jessi whispered back.

"I don't know. That's what I need help with."

Jessi took another bite of pizzaburger. "Hmm," she said. "Do you want to *do* something to them? Do you want to get them in trouble?"

I shook my head. "I really don't know."

As it turned out, it didn't matter. I didn't need plans. That was because of what happened next. Jessi and I were sitting in silence, both planning revenge, when from the next table, I heard my name. The girls were talking about me.

"Jessi," I said quietly, barely moving a muscle, "*don't* look over at Nan and everyone, but they're talking about me. I think."

Immediately Jessi glanced over at the other table.

"I said not to look!" I hissed.

Jessi turned back to me. "They're looking at us," she reported.

"Well, just keep eating. But don't talk. Let's listen to them."

Jessi nodded.

I concentrated on the other table and heard Janet say, "He must have done *some*thing. Something bad."

"Maybe he's stupid," said Rachel, and the four of them giggled.

"Nah," said Nan White finally. "Mallory's father is just a loser."

I gaped at Jessi. She was gaping back at me. "If you don't do something to them," said Jessi, "then I will."

"Don't worry. I'll take care of them," I replied, and stood up.

"You're going to *fight* them?" squeaked Jessi.

"Of course not. There are four of them and only two of us. But watch."

I placed myself at the end of Nan's table. Nan was on my left and Janet on my right. Next to Nan was Rachel. Next to Janet was Valerie. The four of them looked up at me.

"In case you're blind or something," I began, "I just thought I'd tell you that I'm sitting right over there." I pointed to the empty seat across from Jessi. "I also thought I'd tell you that I'm not deaf. I heard everything you said about my father. I suppose you wanted me to, didn't you?" (Nan opened her mouth to say something, but I cut her off.) "That's just the kind of thing people like you would do."

"People like us?" said Valerie uncertainly.

"Yeah. Prejudiced people. But I want you to know that you can talk about me all you want. You can make jokes about me and my family. You can tease me. I don't care. And you know why? Because you're not my real friends, so your opinions don't count. I found out who my real friends are," I went on. "They're the ones who stuck by me when Dad lost his job. It didn't matter to them whether my father was employed. And by the way — not that it's any of your business — my father was not fired because he wasn't doing his job. He was let go, along with a lot of other people in his company, because the business was failing, which was not my father's fault. So go ahead. Say whatever you want. But you guys," I said to Valerie and Rachel, "are not my friends anymore, and *you* guys," (Nan and Janet) "never *were* my friends." I looked back to Rachel and Valerie. "One more thing. Nan White and Janet O'Neal probably aren't *your*

111

true friends, either. They can't be. They don't know how. They're only friends with people when it's convenient for them. So watch out."

Very casually I returned to my lunch and sat down at the table. I couldn't help looking at Valerie and everyone, though. And they were looking back at me, stunned. They were literally speechless, which also meant they didn't apologize to me, but I hadn't expected that anyway.

"Mallory!" Jessi said with a gasp as I slid into my chair. "I can't believe you just did that."

"Neither can I," I replied. And suddenly I found that I was shaking. But I did not regret what I had done. I knew that I had made my point. Rachel and Valerie probably would never talk to me again. But I knew they wouldn't ridicule me, either.

The next afternoon, I went to the Delaneys' once again. And once again, I arrived before Max and Amanda returned from school. When they did, they burst through the front door and Amanda called, "Mallory! Mallory! Where are you? Guess what?"

"I'm right here," I called, hurrying through the hallway from the kitchen, where I'd fixed a snack for the three of us. "What's up?"

Amanda, grinning, flung herself at me. "Your idea worked. Max tried it, too, didn't you, Max?"

"Yup," he answered.

"We told our friends no swimming when a baby-sitter is in charge. And then I invited Angie and Karen and Cici and Meghan to come over this afternoon and play Snail on our driveway."

"And I invited Timmy and Huck to come shoot baskets," added Max.

"And everyone is coming except Angie," Amanda reported. "Even Karen, and her mother has to drive her over."

"Why isn't Angie coming?" I asked. I had helped the kids put away their school things, and now we were seated at the kitchen table, drinking milk and eating oatmeal cookies.

"She said she didn't want to," Amanda replied. "Wasn't that rude?"

I nodded.

"But I didn't like her much anyway. And just like you said, I found out who my real friends are. Max did, too. They're the ones who will come over to play with us even if they can't use the pool."

"Right." I grinned.

The guests began arriving before the kitchen was even cleaned up. First came the neighborhood kids, followed by Karen Brewer. Karen's mother dropped her off and waved to her as she drove away.

The boys had immediately separated themselves from the girls. They were at one end of the driveway playing basketball, while the girls were at the other end (but not too near the street) drawing the diagram for the Snail game.

The seven kids played calmly all afternoon. And no one said a word about the pool, except Amanda, who whispered to me, "Now that I know who my real friends are, I'll tell them the pool rules have changed again. I want to go back in our pool. I miss swimming!"

CHAPTER 13

Friday

Today I sat for Becca and Squirt while Aunt Cecelia went shopping. As always, we had a good time. It was a pretty quiet afternoon. Vanessa and Charlotte came over to play with Becca. Mal, do you know what Vanessa is doing at school to earn money? I guess you probably do. When Becca first told me about it I was surprised, but now I think it's funny.

115

The girls had fun playing Secret Agents (Vanessa taught them the game). And Squirt had fun with his newest activity — climbing stairs! Of course, I have to hold onto him because he's still unsteady. That meant I spent most of the afternoon climbing stairs, too. When we finally stopped I think I was more tired than Squirt was. But sometimes you have to make sacrifices, right?

I certainly did not know what Vanessa had been up to, and when I found out from Jessi *I* was surprised at first, too, and then thought it was funny. Here's how Jessi found out about Vanessa's "job."

It began when Aunt Cecelia was getting ready to leave for an afternoon of shopping. Squirt had just woken up from a nap, and Jessi and Becca had just gotten home from school.

Everyone had gathered in the kitchen.

"Okay, girls," said Aunt Cecelia as she found her pocketbook. "Jessi is in charge while I'm gone." (Duh.) "Becca, listen to your sister." (Doesn't she always?) "I'll be at the mall. You know how to reach your parents or the neighbors if there's an emergency, don't you?"

Of *course* Jessi did. She's a baby-sitter. But all she replied was, "We'll be fine, Aunt Cecelia. Honest."

"All right, then." Jessi's aunt left, looking uncertain.

As soon as they heard her car backing down the driveway, Jessi and Becca looked at each other.

"O-*kay!*" cried Becca. "An afternoon without Aunt Cecelia!"

"Yeah," agreed Jessi. "What do you want for a snack? Since you-know-who isn't here, we can have anything we want."

Becca chose Fig Newtons and juice, and Jessi cut herself a piece of chocolate cake and poured a glass of milk. Then she hoisted Squirt into his high chair and gave him a bottle of juice and some crackers.

"Ah," said Becca, tipping dangerously far back in her chair. "This is the life. I miss having you sit for me, Jessi."

"I miss it, too. But maybe when Aunt Cecelia's been in Stoneybrook longer she'll make friends and start going out more."

Becca suddenly straightened up in her chair. She took a Fig Newton *out* of her mouth. "Oh, no!" she exclaimed.

"What? What's wrong?" asked Jessi. "Is there something in your cookie? Did you lose a tooth?"

"No." Becca had replaced the Fig Newton on her napkin. "I just remembered Vanessa and I felt bad."

"What do you mean?" asked Jessi.

"Doh-bloo!" crowed Squirt from his high chair. His bottle was still in his mouth. Jessi and Becca barely heard him.

"I mean," said Becca, "that Vanessa *never* gets treats like this anymore. You know, because of her father."

Jessi nodded. She did know.

"But maybe she will be able to have treats soon."

"Really? How come?"

"Because she and her brothers and sisters are all earning money."

"Oh, right," said Jessi. "Mal mentioned that to me. But are you saying that Vanessa is actually selling poetry to magazines?"

"Selling poetry to magazines?" repeated Becca. "No. She calls herself Miss Vanessa and styles hair on the playground."

Jessi almost spit out her milk. "Excuse me?

She calls herself Miss Vanessa and styles hair on the playground?"

"Yup," said Becca.

"Is she any good?" asked Jessi, still trying not to laugh.

"I guess. Today she fixed Emma Pape's hair in French braids. Oh, and she also fixed Tess Werner's hair really nicely. Tess just has this plain old brown limp hair, and Vanessa brushed it all over to one side of Tess's head and pulled it into a ponytail. You wouldn't believe what a difference it made."

"Good or bad?" asked Jessi.

"Good, silly," Becca answered, smiling.

"Well, I'm glad for Vanessa," said Jessi.

"Me, too. Some kids have been teasing her about her father. The triplets and Nicky and Margo and even Claire get teased, too."

"Yeah. So does Mallory. . . . Hey, how would you like to invite Vanessa over this afternoon?" Jessi asked her sister.

"Could I?"

"Of course. Go ahead."

So Becca called my house. "Is Miss Vanessa there?" she said when my dad answered the phone, and Jessi laughed.

Vanessa was delighted with her invitation and turned up at the Ramseys' house just twenty minutes later.

"You want to ask Charlotte to come over,

too?" Becca asked Vanessa. (Charlotte Johanssen is Becca's best friend.)

"Okay," replied Vanessa. "I'll teach you guys how to play SAs."

"Essays?" said Becca.

"Yeah. SAs. Secret Agents. It's a really fun game. I'll explain it when Charlotte comes over."

When Jessi told me about SAs, I just groaned. I had hoped my brothers and sisters had forgotten about that game, but apparently they hadn't. SAs is something Jordan invented — a spying game. You need either real or make-believe people to spy on and then the head SA sends the others out on "secret missions." The missions start out easy and get harder. For each mission completed (there are ten in all), you earn a badge. The badges are in different colors — pink for the easiest and black for the hardest. Like a black belt in karate, I guess. Anyway, if you earn all ten badges, you become a top agent.

Vanessa explained this to Becca, Charlotte, and Jessi. Jessi tried to figure out who the girls could spy on, and finally decided not to interfere, except to say, "Don't make nuisances of yourselves. I don't want you looking in the neighbors' windows or anything." Then she turned to Squirt, who was wordlessly demanding to be released from his high chair.

"See you!" Becca called as she and her friends left the kitchen.

"Have fun," Jessi answered. She set Squirt on the floor. "Okay, big guy. What do you want to do this afternoon?"

Squirt couldn't answer in words, but he took Jessi's hand and led her into the front hall. He stopped at the bottom of the staircase.

"You want to climb?" she answered.

"Up," said Squirt, and began climbing. It was a laborious process for him. One slow step at a time. Reaching the top seemed to take forever. As soon as they'd reached the second floor though, Squirt turned around.

"Down," he said solemnly.

Step . . . step . . . step . . . step.

Jessi must be unendingly patient.

They reached the first floor.

"Up," said Squirt.

Oh, brother, thought Jessi.

She and Squirt were halfway upstairs for the second time when Jessi thought she heard a noise behind her. Still gripping Squirt's hand, she looked over her shoulder. Nothing.

Step, step, step, step.

Another noise. Jessi looked again. This time she saw a flash of red disappear around a corner. (Charlotte was wearing a red sweater.)

"Aha," said Jessi to her little brother. "You know what? I think we're being spied on.

Someone has been sent on a secret mission."

"Down," was Squirt's reply.

Jessi helped him turn around — and saw her sister disappear around a corner.

Twenty minutes later, Squirt *finally* tired of climbing the stairs. Jessi took him into the TV room to watch *Sesame Street*. She pretended not to notice when Vanessa peered into the room, wrote something on a notepad, and disappeared.

Jessi was sure that the girls — who were fairly unobtrusive — spied on her and Squirt all afternoon. Her proof came near five o'clock when Charlotte and Vanessa said they had to go home.

"*I*," announced Charlotte proudly, "earned my blue badge. I completed *three* secret missions."

"I completed four," said Becca. "I got my green badge."

"Where are the badges?" asked Jessi.

"Jordan will have to make them. He's the top agent," said Vanessa seriously.

Charlotte left then, and Vanessa looked at Jessi and Becca. "Thank you very much for inviting me over," she said. "I'm really glad you did."

I knew how my sister felt. She was relieved because she still had friends.

Jessi told me later that she'd never seen anyone look as happy as Vanessa did when she climbed on her bike. And I have to say that Vanessa was positively *beaming* when she arrived home.

Vanessa's arrival coincided with a phone call. As usual these days, Dad dashed for the telephone and picked it up after one ring.

"Hello?" he said. Then, "This is he. . . . Yes. . . . Yes, I did. . . . You would? . . . On Tuesday? Of course. That's fine. Thank you very much. Good-bye."

"Dad?" I asked. "Who was that?"

"Only the vice-president of Metro-Works. He wants me to come in for an interview on Tuesday. He saw my résumé and likes it. Also, he talked to my old boss. He got a good recommendation from him."

"Dad, that's fantastic!" I cried. I threw my arms around him.

Dad was smiling, but he said, "Now don't get your hopes up too high. This is just one lead on one job."

"Okay," I said. I immediately called Jessi, though. "Dad has a job lead!" I told her excitedly. "He's got an interview on Tuesday at some place called Metro-Works."

"That's wonderful!" cried Jessi.

"But we can't get our hopes up too high," I said, even though my hopes were already skyrocketing.

CHAPTER 14

Dad's job interview was on Tuesday. I think our entire family was as nervous as Dad was. We felt as if we were sending him off to college or something. I could barely concentrate in school that day. As soon as the final bell rang, I was out the door. I didn't even wait for Jessi so we could walk partway home together. I just made a dash for my house. All the way there, I kept my fingers crossed. I was pretty sure that if I did that, I'd be greeted with good news.

I burst through our front door and dumped all my stuff on the floor.

"Dad! Dad!" I called.

"Mallory?" Dad poked his head out of the kitchen.

"Did you get it?" (I was gasping for breath.)

"Get it? The job?"

"Sure. What else?" I ran into the kitchen.

"Oh, honey, I don't know yet."

"You *don't?*" I said in disappointment. "When *will* you know?"

"I'm not sure. I have to go back for another interview on Thursday."

"Aw, man. That is stale."

Dad grinned at me. "Tired of having an unemployed father?"

I grinned back. "At least you can joke about it now."

On Thursday, Dad went to Metro-Works for his second interview. And I spent another day biting my nails. *This* time when I ran home, I burst through the front door and yelled, "Okay, when do you start?"

Dad, in the kitchen with Claire as usual, gave me a rueful smile. "Maybe sometime after the third interview."

"The *third* interview?" I wailed. "When is *that?*"

"Tomorrow."

"Why do you have to have all of these interviews? Is this a good sign or a bad sign, Dad?"

"A good one. It means they like me. They want all the top people at the firm to meet me."

"Well, why can't they do that all at once? Like the spirits in *A Christmas Carol. They* didn't make *Scrooge* wait for three nights. They all visited him on Christmas Eve so that he wouldn't miss Christmas Day."

Dad laughed. "Maybe Metro-Works likes to torture prospective employees."

"Are you sure you want a job at a place that tortures its workers?"

"Don't look a gift horse in the mouth," was Dad's reply.

(I had to call Kristy to ask her what that means. Kristy's stepfather is the King of Clichés. I knew that Kristy would be able to explain the gift horse thing. She said it means don't turn down an offer you really need, or something like that. So I relaxed about the third interview.)

On Friday, unfortunately, I wasn't able to tear home from school. I had to go to the Delaneys' and then to a BSC meeting. But I bolted out of that meeting before Claud's clock changed to 6:01, and made it home in a record seven minutes. The second I entered the house I knew the outcome of the third interview. My entire family was gathered in the living room.

They were all smiling.

"You got it, didn't you, Dad?" I whispered.

He nodded.

I let out a whoop. Then I hugged Dad. And the next thing I knew, everyone was hugging everyone else. And Claire was saying, "Now I can get Skipper!"

"Tell me about it," I said to Dad when we were sitting down again.

"Well," Dad began, "I'll be a lawyer for Metro-Works. The job is similar to my old one. It's not *quite* as big, and the salary is slightly lower, but I might have a chance for a promotion next year. To make up the difference in pay," he went on, "your mother may continue doing temporary work. We'll figure out baby-sitting arrangements some other time."

"Right now," said Mom, "we're going to have a celebration. A nice family dinner. . . . Cooked by your father."

My brothers and sisters and I exchanged glances.

"Cooked by Dad?" repeated Adam.

"Hey, I'm a pretty good cook now," Dad said defensively. "Let's see. I made all your favorite things: cabbage, squash, Brussels sprouts — "

"Oh, gross. I'm gonna blow cookies!" shrieked Adam.

"Adam!" Mom admonished him. (She hates when Adam says "blow cookies.")

"Really, Dad. What did you make for dinner?" asked Nicky.

"Hamburgers, baked potatoes, and salad."

"And I believe we have a special dessert," added Mom.

"All *right!*" said Jordan.

Fifteen minutes later we were seated in the dining room. We never eat there except on Thanksgiving and Christmas, or if our grandparents come over. Even though the meal was just hamburgers, Mom had set the table with silverware, our good china, a white tablecloth, and white linen napkins.

When we had been served, Byron said, "Dad? When do you start your new job?"

"A week from Monday," replied Dad. "And now that I've found a job, I think I can relax a little. I really enjoy being at home."

"That's good," I said. "We were worried about you."

"We were worried about a lot of things," said Vanessa.

"That's why Mallory helped us form the Pike Club. Right, Mal?"

"Right," I replied, and then had to explain what the Pike Club was. (My brothers and sisters and I decided to keep meeting from time to time.)

"Tell me what you worried about," said Mom.

"Money, mostly," said Margo. "We were afraid we'd lose our home."

"Lose our home!" exclaimed Dad.

"Yeah," said Claire. " 'Cause of the baggage."

"She means mortgage," said Jordan. "Mallory said that the bank owns part of our house, and each month we have to pay the bank back some money."

"And that if we couldn't pay the bank, they'd take our house away," said Margo.

"Well, that *is* true," agreed Dad, "and I'm sure that some people become homeless that way. But we wouldn't have had that problem. I was getting severance pay from the old company. Whenever an employee is fired, his firm is required to pay him his salary for awhile after he or she leaves."

The triplets shot me a dirty look.

"Well, I didn't *know* that," I said to them.

"You made me do all that work!" cried Jordan.

"I didn't make you. You agreed to."

Mom spoke up. "I want you kids to know how proud your father and I are of you. You handled this situation very well."

"Thanks," I said. "It wasn't always easy."

"I know. You worked hard to earn your money."

"Oh, it wasn't just the money. We had trouble at school."

"Yeah," said Adam.

"Trouble?" asked Dad. "You all brought home the same good grades as usual."

"Not that kind of trouble," Vanessa told our parents. "It was the kids at school. They . . . they, um — "

"They were mean," said Claire.

"They were?" asked Dad.

"Yeah. They teased us when we didn't have money for trips or to buy lunch at school. That kind of thing," said Byron.

"And some kids went beyond teasing," I added. I told Mom and Dad about Nan White, Janet O'Neal, and Valerie and Rachel.

"Valerie and Rachel?" said Mom. "I thought they — "

"I know, I know. You thought they were my friends. So did I. But, boy, I found out who my real friends are. I found out a few other things, too."

"Hmm," said Dad. "Maybe I should lose my job more often."

"No way!" cried Claire.

There was a pause. Then Mom said, "You kids were certainly enterprising."

"We were what?" asked Margo.

"Enterprising. That means you had good ideas about how to earn money."

"Well, I don't think I was *terribly* enterprising," I replied. "I've been baby-sitting all along. The only difference was that I gave you my money."

"I think *we* were enterprising," said Byron, speaking for the triplets.

"Yeah. We got a lot of calls for ABJ." Adam looked pretty pleased with himself. "We walked dogs, we weeded gardens. We even painted all of Dawn Schafer's mother's lawn chairs."

"We're going to keep ABJ going," added Jordan.

"I'm going to stick with my paper route," said Nicky.

"I can't believe he *got* a paper route," muttered Adam.

Since I was sitting next to Adam I felt that it was okay to kick him under the table. He was just miffed because Nicky, two years younger than the triplets and working alone, had managed to earn more money than all of ABJ. And the triplets are always telling Nicky what a dweeb he is. But he had shown them a thing or two, without even planning on it.

"CM was a good idea, too, wasn't it?" Claire asked.

"It was very good," said Mom.

"We only earned eleven dollars and sixty cents, though," said Margo. "That's not too much. We sold lemonade *and* brownies. But not many people came to our stand."

"You tried, though," spoke up Dad. "That's what counts."

"Vanessa," said Mom, "you've been awfully quiet. Did you really earn all that money selling poetry? If you did, I'd sort of like to see it published. What magazines bought it?"

Vanessa blushed the color of a tomato. As far as she knew, *nobody* was aware that she'd been Miss Vanessa at school, not even the triplets, Nicky, Margo, and Claire, who *go* to her school.

"Um . . . well . . . I — I — " Vanessa stammered.

All heads turned toward her.

"I didn't exactly publish my poetry," Vanessa managed to say.

"You didn't?" said Mom.

"No. I . . . "

I could tell that Vanessa just wasn't going to be able to tell about Miss Vanessa, so I did it for her. I tried to make her sound talented and important, but there was a lot of snickering anyway.

Mom and Dad, however, refrained from even smiling.

"Very enterprising," said Mom smartly.

"Very . . . creative," added Dad.

"Maybe Vanessa will own a beauty school when she grows up," said Adam, spluttering in an attempt not to laugh out loud. I took the opportunity to kick him again. And that was the end of the teasing.

Dinner ended, and Mom said, "Okay, time for dessert."

"All *right!*" exclaimed Nicky.

"Is it junk food?" I asked hopefully.

"Practically," Mom replied. She disappeared into the kitchen and reappeared with a cake. A gooey, thick, chocolately *bakery* cake on which was written in bright yellow icing: CONGRATULATIONS!

Fifteen minutes later, the cake was gone. (Well, there *are* ten of us.)

When the table had been cleared and the kitchen cleaned up, Mom said, "Let's continue our celebration. How about home movies and videos?"

"With popcorn?" asked Claire.

"Sure. We can make popcorn."

So we did. Then my family — Mom, Dad, my brothers, my sisters, and I — gathered in the rec room. First we ran the movie projector. We watched films of Mom and Dad at their wedding, then standing in front of their first house, and then standing next to their first car. ("What a bomb!" hooted Jordan.) Then we watched movies of me drooling, the triplets eating in a row of high chairs, Vanessa painting at an easel, and the five of us putting on a "fashion show." After that, we switched to videos. There were Nicky, Margo, and Claire dressed for Easter, a Christmas morning with Mom and all of us kids tearing into presents, and more.

When I went to bed that night, I relaxed immediately and slept without dreaming.

CHAPTER 15

"P̲ar-*ty!*" yelled Stacey.

I giggled. It was a Saturday night. Stacey, Dawn, and Mary Anne were standing on my front stoop. I was hosting the first ever BSC sleepover at *my* house. We've had plenty of sleepovers at Kristy's house, and the houses of the older members, but never at Jessi's or my house. I felt a little nervous about this, but mostly I was excited. Apparently Stacey was excited, too.

"Come on down to the rec room," I said. "We have to sleep there because there isn't enough space in Vanessa's and my bedroom."

Dawn, Mary Anne, and Stacey followed me downstairs. They spread out their sleeping bags. (Mine was already unrolled.)

It was six o'clock. By six-thirty, all seven of us were in the rec room, sitting on our sleeping bags.

"So what's to eat?" asked Claud. "I'm starved."

"Dad's bringing us hoagie sandwiches. He's picking them up on his way home from work," I replied.

"Oh, yeah," said Stacey, who was emptying a bag of makeup and nail polish into her lap. "How's his job going?"

"He likes it," I told her. "He says the people are really nice. It's not exactly the same as his old job, though."

"But he's not out of work," Jessi reminded me.

"That," I replied, "is definitely the best part. Mom's only temping once or twice a week now."

"Mal?" asked Mary Anne. "Is — "

Squish, squish.

"Ew!" squeaked Kristy. "I've been slimed! Gross."

Kristy's shirt sported a streak of gooey green slime across the front.

"Adam!" I yelled.

No answer. I turned to Kristy. "Don't worry. The slime is sort of like shampoo. It'll wash out. It won't leave a stain."

"But what happened?" asked Kristy.

"Adam got you with his Power-X Slime-Master Gun," I said.

My friends laughed. But I wasn't about to let the triplets spoil my first slumber party. "Adam!" I yelled again. "Byron! Jordan!"

"Maybe it was Nicky," suggested Dawn.

"No, I'm pretty sure it was Adam. . . . Hey, Adam, if — "

Squish, squish.

"Yikes! Slimed again!" cried Claudia. "And this time it's in my hair."

"That does it," I said as Claud and Kristy headed into the bathroom to wash out the Power-X slime.

I was about to run upstairs and find Adam when the door to the garage opened and in strode Dad with —

"Food!" exclaimed Claud, emerging from the bathroom.

Dad greeted us and doled out the hoagies before he even took his coat off. Then I complained to him about Adam and the slime and Dad promised to "see to things." He sounded sort of threatening.

When we had settled down with sandwiches and sodas, Kristy said, "Well, I sat for Amanda and Max this afternoon."

"How are they?" I asked. (My month-long job was over and I hadn't seen the Delaneys in a week or so.)

"Fine," said Kristy.

"Any pool trouble?" I asked.

Kristy smiled. "Nope. You solved that problem. I saw it with my own eyes. Amanda invited Karen over to play, and Max invited Huck over. Karen and Huck both brought their suits with them, but when they saw that Amanda and Max weren't wearing *their* suits, they didn't say a word. They behaved like good guests."

"Maybe they've read *Uncle Roland, the Perfect Guest*," said Mary Anne, and the rest of us laughed. (It's a really funny picture book for little kids.)

"Did any kids show up uninvited?" I asked Kristy, with a mouthful of ham and cheese. (I'll never again take junk food for granted.)

"Nope," Kristy answered. "I think there may have been a change in pool rules."

"Well, Amanda and Max realized they couldn't buy friends," I said. I paused. Then I said, "Hey, you'll never guess what happened this afternoon."

"What?" asked everyone.

"*Rachel* called me."

"*Rachel?*" cried Jessi. "That toadhead?"

"Yes. Rachel the toadhead. You know what? She'd heard about our party tonight and she didn't exactly come out and *ask* to be invited, but I know that's what she wanted. I think Valerie might have been with her. Rachel kept covering up the phone and whispering to somebody."

"What did you say to her?" Stacey wanted to know.

"I made it very clear that the party was for my *friends*. And Rachel got all sweet-sounding and said something about our silly fight and how it was all in the past. And I said, 'Because my father has a job again?' and Rachel didn't say anything, so I told her to go call Nan or Janet. Then I hung up on her. I actually hung — "

"Hey!" Kristy interrupted. "I just got an idea. Let's goof call Nan White and Janet O'Neal later. They deserve it."

"Okay," I said, giggling. "Should we do Sam's favorite?"

"Yes," was Kristy's immediate reply. "And then we'll do a pig farm call."

"A pig farm call?" Jessi and I repeated at the same time.

"You'll see," Mary Anne told us.

We finished our supper, cleaned up our trash, and then stood around the phone in the kitchen. We all knew what Sam's favorite goof call was.

"Who should call first?" asked Dawn. "And who are we goofing?"

"We're goofing Nan," Kristy replied immediately, "because she's worse than Janet and this is a more annoying call. And anyone except Mallory can call her first. I think Mal should make the last call."

"I'll go first, then," said Jessi, and she picked up the phone and dialed Nan's private number. "Hello, is Sissy there?" she asked. She paused. "There isn't?" she said innocently. "There's no Sissy there?" Then she hung up and we doubled over laughing.

During the next half an hour, Kristy, Stacey, Mary Anne, Claudia, and Dawn each called Nan and asked for Sissy. Dawn reported that Nan sounded especially angry after her call.

"Good," I said, and picked up the phone.

"What *is* it?" cried Nan when she answered.

"This is Sissy," I said. "Have there been any calls for me?"

"Mallory Pike?" exclaimed Nan. "Is that you?"

"No, it's Sissy," I said. I hung up and exploded into laughter.

"All right, now it's Janet's turn," said Kristy. "Who'll make the pig farm call?"

To everyone's surprise, Mary Anne said, "I will." Then she added, "I've got Logan's southern accent down pat." (A southern accent seemed to be crucial to a pig farm call.)

We had to look Janet's number up in the phone book. When we found it, Mary Anne dialed it and said (in her regular voice) to whomever had answered the phone, "Hello, is Janet there, please?" A few moments later, Mary Anne put on her accent. "Hello, Mizz O'Neal?" she drawled. "This is Mizz Patterson from Atlanta Pig Farm. The two hundred piglets you ordered are ready. How would you like them shipped to you?"

Well, of course, Janet must have said something like, "I don't know anything about pigs from a pig farm."

So Mary Anne, who ordinarily is a terrible, unconvincing liar, made her voice all trembly and insisted, "But you *did* order them. I've got the form right in front of me. Two hundred piglets for a Mizz Janet O'Neal in Stoneybrook, Connecticut."

I don't know what Janet said to that, but for the next ten minutes or so Mary Anne became more and more upset, saying that her boss would fire her if she didn't put through the order and collect the two thousand dollars that Janet owed Atlanta Pig Farm. When Mary Anne finally got off the phone, having told Janet that she was sure to lose her job, she was actually crying, and the rest of us were laughing so hard we'd had to run to the rec room and get pillows to put over our faces, so that Janet wouldn't hear us.

"Well, I guess we got *them* back," I said, referring to Nan and Janet, and feeling deeply satisfied.

The seven of us returned to the rec room.

"Make-over time!" announced Stacey.

"No, let's raid the refrigerator," said Claud.

"Raid the refrigerator! We just ate," Jessi pointed out.

I was about to suggest phoning Nan again and asking if there'd been any more calls for Sissy, when Dad appeared in the rec room. He handed me something. It was the Power-X Slime-Master Gun.

"Here, my enterprising daughter," he said. "I found this hidden under the sink in the upstairs bathroom. See if you can put it to good use."

I grinned. "Thanks, Dad." Then I said to my friends as Dad was leaving, "Well, I guess we know what to do with this."

"Yup," said everyone.

So we staged a sneak slime attack on the triplets in their bedroom. Then we returned to our sleeping bags. We talked and ate and told each other our dreams and fears. I didn't sleep a wink.

It was one of the best nights of my life.

About the Author

ANN M. MARTIN did *a lot* of baby-sitting when she was growing up in Princeton, New Jersey. Now her favorite baby-sitting charge is her cat, Mouse, who lives with her in her Manhattan apartment.

Ann Martin's Apple Paperbacks are *Bummer Summer, Inside Out, Stage Fright, Me and Katie (the Pest)*, and all the other books in the Baby-sitters Club series.

She is a former editor of books for children, and was graduated from Smith College. She likes ice cream, the beach, and *I Love Lucy*; and she hates to cook.

Look for #40

CLAUDIA AND THE
MIDDLE SCHOOL MYSTERY

I stood outside the bathroom door for about thirty seconds, trying to figure out what Nancy Drew would do if she were in my shoes. Then I slowly pushed the door open and peeked inside.

There are four stalls in that bathroom. Three of them were occupied by Shawna and her friends. Quickly, before I could change my mind, I slipped into the fourth.

The toilet next to mine flushed right then, and I heard someone walk over to the sink. The water ran for a minute. Then I heard a girl say, "Shawna, I swear. You are so lucky." She was chewing gum loudly. That must be the one with the red hair, I thought.

"I know," said Shawna, who had just come out of *her* stall. "I still can't believe I got away with it." She giggled. "I just gave Mr. Zorzi this incredibly sincere, honest look — and he let me go!"

I couldn't believe what I was hearing. Were they actually talking about what it *seemed* like they were talking about? I was suddenly terrified that they would find out I was eavesdropping on them. I held my breath and tried to get my heart to stop beating so loudly. I kept listening. This was exactly what I wanted to hear.